Speculations

Stories

I0621153

M.V. Montgomery

Winter Goose Publishing

BOOKS BY M.V. MONTGOMERY

POETRY

Joshu Holds a Press Conference (2010)

Strange Conveyances (2010)

What We Did With Old Moons (2012)

A Dictionary of Animal Symbols (2014)

FICTION

Dream Koans (2011)

Antigravitas (2011)

Beyond the Pale (2013)

Winter Goose Publishing
2701 Del Paso Road, 130-92
Sacramento, CA 95835

www.wintergoosepublishing.com
Contact Information: info@wintergoosepublishing.com

Speculations

COPYRIGHT © 2015 by M.V. Montgomery

First Edition, February 2015

Cover Art by Winter Goose Publishing
Photograph by Paul Nine-O
Typesetting by Odyssey Books

ISBN: 978-1-941058-24-4

Published in the United States of America

*To my father, D.E. Montgomery,
and to all my literary fathers*

CONTENTS

Speculations

A BRIEF HISTORY OF VIGILISM

Jazmin Garcia-Kendall's recent book *A Brief History of Vigilism* (Thune Press, $24.95) chronicles that odd coalition of social psychologists, artists, and therapists who banded together circa 1983. Famously, the Vigilists argued that the Voyager probe, having outlasted its original mission of completing flybys of Jupiter and Saturn, rather than doubling down on Uranus and Neptune, should be reprogrammed instead to "turn around." Why not point that telescope back at Earth to learn more about ourselves? And if not Voyager 1, why not Voyager 2?

Although this proposal was not considered seriously at NASA, what the Vigilists hoped to learn was both simple and complex. The short answer is that the group simply placed great psychological value on distant images of Earth. We commonly picture a planet against a backdrop of stars, but have a personal stake in the cosmos when that planet is our own.

The Vigilist group held brief sway as a lobby, gaining traction on university campuses, where the young Garcia-Kendall, then a sophomore at Berkeley, first encountered them. She admits to becoming enamored of some of their more idealistic notions, such as the proposal to telecast Earth images minus political boundaries worldwide to send out the message "We Are One."

A noble sentiment? Perhaps. But one totally out of synch with the getting-and-spending Reagan years.

***

In order to gain entrée into the scientific community, the Vigilists were compelled to make a radically different case.

Light travels at 186,300 miles per second; the moon is 238,900 miles from the Earth. Images of our planet seen from the moon are therefore always 1.3 seconds in the past. To capture those images and beam them back to Earth entails a total time delay of about three seconds.

Thus, if we wished to revisit very recent moments, we could. We might arrange a delayed feed on a billboard or Jumbotron above a city street, for instance. A record of unfolding events would be there to consult if we felt we'd just missed out on an important bit of information or intriguing detail.

Farther out in space, beyond the reach of the most powerful Earth-bound telescopes, light particles disperse like pixels vanishing from a photograph. If we could account for some of this randomization with predictive models, adjusting for atmospheric distortion, the Vigilists contended that we could, theoretically, see into the more distant past.

Instead of a three-second delay, how about a three-minute delay? This would allow us to moderate our social behavior, relocate lost pets and children, or summon police to get a fresh look at a crime scene or perpetrator.

And what if a string of satellites, stretching still further into the cosmos, retrieved information from the previous three months or three years? We could relive moments that had made a lasting impact on our lives. Cold cases could be reopened and battlefields scrutinized for war crimes. We'd have no choice but to own our history and live with it.

Though outlandish, these Vigilist scenarios nonetheless presage the way, thirty-odd years later, the private has become public. To demonstrate how addictive watching ourselves on a live feed can be, Garcia-Kendall draws analogies to social media sites like Twitter and Snapchat. Increasingly, we've become performers, choosing actions for their propensity to generate a brief text or video highlight rather than for practical reasons.

True, we may deploy smartphones in socially useful ways, to collect data or even to police ourselves (as the Vigilists predicted). But the studies Garcia-Kendall cites confirm the comparatively weak appeal of pointing the cameras outward, in the face of our constant compulsion to turn them inward.

The Vigilists didn't extend their arguments any further because they could not have foreseen how Voyager would outlast its five-year mission by more than sevenfold. But what if we could reassemble the photon-pixels dating back three hundred years? Three thousand? We'd then be in a position to examine the founding myths of most nations and religions.

All of which sounds far-fetched, until we recall that Earthbound telescopes presently retrieve images from the creation of galaxies and capture neutrinos set in motion by the Big Bang.

As of this writing, Voyager is approximately 11.6 billion miles from the sun. Unfortunately, even if we were to heed the lost call of the Vigilists to "turn it around," its camera requires too long an exposure to send back any pictures of Earth at all—even the most distant ones.

DANIEL L. ERST, INVENTOR OF THE MULTIVERSE HELMET

The human genome contains more noncoding strands of DNA than necessary ones; the brain has more storage capacity than ever gets used; and the cosmos is replete with mysterious dark matter. We are taught to believe that space is mostly empty, but often, a contrary premise holds equally true . . . considered from an alternative perspective, the universe's essential condition is wretched excess. Such were the reflections of Daniel L. Erst, Ph.D., late inventor of the multiverse helmet.

The night he conceived of his invention, Erst was at home in Ventura, California, staring at a picture on his desk of his soon to be ex-wife, Diana Stebbins Erst. Diana had left Erst earlier that day to take a teaching position in another city, and in conversations over the weeks leading up to the decisive loading of the moving van, he'd wondered what he wasn't saying or doing correctly in order to avert this catastrophe. A blank page in his typewriter, Erst was still trying to make his case to the absent Diana, and still not succeeding.

To this point in his life, Erst was not what anyone

would call a lateral thinker. A former physicist, he spent weary days as a community college teacher while his theoretical interests lay fallow in vast veldts of untilled brain. It wasn't always so: Diana, a former pupil and protégé, once used the word "enthralling" to describe conversations of the early days, which had featured more back-and-forth than the marriage itself.

Erst sensed a lack too, but when he attempted to talk to her, could never seem to think of the right thing to say.

First and Second Insights (1976)

Now as he regarded the picture of Diana, Erst was on verge of discovering his celebrated *Insights*.

To start off his letter, he'd searched for an opening phrase expressive of his state of mind. As usual, he'd drawn a blank. His agitation was such that merely typing "Dear Diana" was too much, for it immediately gave him cause to reflect that yes, she was just that—dear. He tried typing "Dear Diana" over and over until a clause somehow managed to squeeze itself out. *Perhaps in another universe, we shall remain together*, Erst wrote, and then stopped.

Another universe. How many were there?—he'd

forgotten. He glanced around as if expecting to discover a portal right there in his living room. Given his present emotional state, if he *had* seen one, he would have stepped right through it.

A happier Erst, and many happier Erst-Diana pairs must exist elsewhere, he lamented. Yet at the same time, it didn't seem plausible to him that his pain could be replicated, nor could the multiplied sorrows of a dozen parallel Ersts ever add up to anything worse than what he felt at present.

In a sudden surge of emotion, he thought the whole idea of parallel universes inauthentic—and even worse (to a scientist), unnecessary. He felt his heart brimming with enough angst and dark matter to supply a dozen failed relationships.

Fortunately for history, Erst chose that moment to remove the Diana page from his typewriter and insert another. On it, he pursued his new line of thinking.

There is no difference between psychological and material phenomena, he considered. The mind cannot be greater than the brain. What would we see right now, if we ran an MRI scan on Erst? Due to his depression, no doubt an extraordinarily low level of cognitive functioning. But what sort of picture would emerge if we viewed his brain on the subatomic level? Surely, a dazzling amount of energy. This activity must approach the "thought" threshold continually, if not in one's own head, perhaps in an alternative field, one lying simultaneously "within and without."

Those incipient thought waves had to go somewhere. It was folly to think a human skull some type of an ion-tight container.

And thus Erst's First Insight: *Thought is independent of the brain.*

The brain is an organ for the reception of thought in the same way an ear receives sound, but thought by nature is *multiversal*, by which Erst meant it coexists among, or "transverses," more than one field of consciousness.

Solipsism is a logical impossibility; we can never fully "embody" a thought wave or control its reception. Indeed, what we often mistake for original inspiration is, upon further examination, simply environmental influence, what was in the air at the time. We are deluded into believing ourselves the agents of thought rather than its vessels.

Erst's Second Insight followed hard-upon: *Because*

the universe is multiple, thought waves occupy different dimensions simultaneously.

A thought, like light (reasoned Erst), is both wave and particle. In the context of an individual brain scan, we detect "hot" areas of activity and branching strands. But in a more approximate, subatomic reading, we encounter a more diffuse energy field, as particles implicated in cognitive activity dance their dances both inside and *outside* of the brain pan.

Famously, Erst pulled out his Occam's razor. He considered the common *déjà vu* feeling one gets— how a time delay slows the processing of an event so that the present is perceived as past; i.e., one has lived through it before. It would be less operose to posit that the thought registers simultaneously *elsewhere*.

So, too, with memories: the cause of their notorious inaccuracy is not so much their diminution over time, but rather, their tendency to "spill over" into multiple fields of consciousness comprising discrete patterns of association.

And just so with various opposing, partial, or confused ideas: these are the result of *multiversal overloads* of organic energy.

The above is a cleaned-up version of Insight Number 2. That first night, Erst's thinking was all over the place.

Prototype and Early Modification Period (1976-7)

Early the next day, Erst was at work in his half-empty garage. His eventual prototype was a refurbished motorcycle helmet bound with cable wires designed to both "contain and control": to insulate thought waves against environmental distractions, and to prevent their escape into other folds of consciousness.

The mock-up proved unsuccessful, causing excess joules of electrostatic energy to fire off a volley of ear-splitting synapses. Erst's cortex lit up like a battlefield at night.

The experience was not, as some might hold, akin to a schizophrenic's hearing multiple voices; it was more a case of having too many half-formed notions to follow, with the added obstacle of a whanging migraine; and later, upon removal of the helmet, a marked state of dullness and aporia in the subject, who felt like a video gamer overstimulated after an all-nighter.

A hasty adjustment to the helmet introduced a filtering device which allowed for selective tuning of keener thought waves. The result was a primitive "expansion of consciousness," albeit to a moderate degree.

During the Early Modification period, Erst discovered a nascent ability to isolate alternate timelines and project them, crudely, into the near future. He was able to discern alternate scenarios for his life—which now, thanks to the helmet, became more sharply defined. In particular, he saw how things might have gone differently with Diana. Too late, he thought of witty rejoinders and mots justes that might have rescued him.

He had the idea to send Diana a card to ask how she was doing, then a subsequent idea that he should follow up on the first one to better enhance his chances for success, so he did (send the card). The outcome was a phone chat Diana later characterized as "not entirely distressing."

Further improvements in helmet design led to a reduction of post-trial side effects. Here it must be noted later test subjects experimenting with Erst's original prototype reported far fewer symptoms in the first place. It's been suggested Erst may have been a lifelong sufferer of a rare syndrome known as EMF (ElectroMagnetic Field) Sensitivity.

The visions the scientist received of potential futures via the new helmet were clearer, yet tended to dissipate quickly, leaving him a short window in which to record his observations. Erst could see himself in a renewed career as a physicist, for example; or like Diana, landing a teaching job in another city. In most dimensions, he and Diana were reunited, although in at least one, he found himself locked in the embrace of an enchanting young black woman on an island resembling Barbados or Bermuda—until this travelogue abruptly faded. After the session, rather shamefacedly, Erst set the helmet aside and tromped to his desk to stare at his ex-wife's picture until he'd refreshed her image in his brain.

When it came right down to it, Erst couldn't be entirely sure he was experiencing events in another field of consciousness, versus merely projecting his repressed fantasies into the future, to be augmented by the multiverse helmet in the way a bigger antenna enhanced a TV image.

He held no illusions anyone's life events were "predetermined"; on the contrary, he'd discovered that one course of action might appear attractive for the short-term, but when traced to its logical end, dim, or be overrun by previously unforeseen circumstances. What Erst needed to ascertain was whether the alternate timelines could be used to predict outcomes with greater than fifty percent accuracy. He wished to feel more certain of things; and of course, of Diana.

In the meantime, while trying to get the helmet right, he dared not share his discoveries for fear he'd be perceived as some kind of nutjob with a colander on his head.

Late Modification Period (1977-8)

The second series of upgrades to the multiverse helmet supplied much needed battery power and introduced *sequencing*, which revealed more of the scaffolding needed to actively build toward a life goal and helped predict short term futures with spectacular fifty-seven percent accuracy. For this latter reason, the Second Modification helmet, or "Quicken" as it is known to devotees, remains popular at tradeshows and Comic Con.

The modified device finally gave Erst the sought-for lucidity, allowing him to preview life-decisions and see how they were likely to play out for years to come—as many as fourteen years, it's been claimed, although this figure varies widely based on the course of action chosen, risk ratios, and user.

In less than one year, Erst accumulated virtual experiences comparable to several lifetimes, and also made more than a few inroads toward a reunion with Diana. She proved a hard sell, but he sent ideas for vacations together; witty, somewhat self-deprecating remarks regarding his own past shortcomings (those took the words right out of her mouth); and heartfelt suggestions for building a life together centered around family and children—all of which measurably scored points with her.

Diana couldn't help thinking Erst had regained much of his former brilliance, perhaps even more, and that it might actually prove stimulating to be around this guy. True, she had a job in a new city and didn't see how things could work. But each time she thought to raise an objection, Erst took a short intermission and came back with a proposal for working around the problem that was, at the same time, elegant and simple.

Further Refinements (1977-83)

Erst discovers during this extended trial-and-error period that multiversal decisions have effects farther reaching than at first thought and/or generate unforeseen "subplots" which may leave messy traces. Further helmet adjustments are made to smooth virtual timeline wrinkles—briefly flitting doubts, social gaffes and glitches, moments of unrest.

Although we'll never know precisely what this pioneer might have foreseen of mankind's future (perhaps in *conjunction with* his own life, since his importance to posterity is assured), we begin to detect some contrarian signs of Erst's growing indifference towards his professional work.

The multiverse helmet appears to lose its novelty for him. When he finally submits his *Insights* to physics journals, he does so in a characteristically casual, perfunctory way.

Yet paradoxically, Erst's existential crisis has a joyous outcome: Diana's concerned knock on his door. Soon the two have fully reconciled.

Oddly, Erst didn't see that one coming.

Six years later, the Ersts are a family of four: Daniel, Diana, and a boy and baby girl. A serious-faced little man who tries on his dad's "space helmet" and boasts about becoming an astronaut, and a tousle-headed little darlin' Erst loves to bounce on his knee while humming Tex Ritter tunes.

Erst would've been the first one to tell you he didn't

see either of them coming, either.

New Explorations: Helmet to Helmet (1996)

Over the years, Erst often complained of headaches. It's speculated that his EMF Sensitivity might have indicated an underlying condition such as an intracranial aneurysm. But this diagnosis was never borne out by evidence; and while a full autopsy was never performed upon Erst's body prior to cremation, there's no reason to question the official cause of death, which is "anaphylactic shock ensuing from a snake bite."

Before this tragedy would occur on his beloved daily hike—indeed, for many long, happy years—Erst actively shared all of his findings with his life partner Diana Stebbins Erst, their collaboration leading to one last, great breakthrough in multiverse theory.

Erst's New Theory of Simultaneity (1996) holds that since thoughts transcend the individual, they have the potential to become *transpersonal*, i.e., held in tandem by more than one subject at a time.

Materialist explanations would follow for compatibility, synchronicity, empathy and other phenomena. Linked-helmet trials were conducted to allow paired subjects to experience thought waves simultaneously—although by this point, Erst's interest in the field was purely theoretical.

For a while, the Nobel Committee could have gone either way, Physics or Peace, given the new helmet's potential to promote understanding between individuals, hence unity among nations (it went with Physics, in 2001).

The Third Modification helmet, nicknamed the "Amity," proved a marketable commodity, especially among newlyweds and couples looking to put a little za-zing back into their relationship. For an extra thousand dollars, a new polymer catch basin feature could be added, along with EDS (Enhanced Dual Streaming).

During this period, many TV networks clamored for interviews with Erst, or even better, Daniel and Diana together. When an initial round of offers failed to arouse interest, one station proposed giving the "sci-wise" couple its own show.

Yet for some unknown reason, the Ersts chose this moment to abandon the limelight, grab the kids, and move to Arizona.

And that's about all the public knows of their story.

Post Mortem (2015)

Before closing this account of the contributions of Daniel L. Erst, Ph.D., it may not be overstepping the bounds to offer a brief comment on one or two issues which have arisen since the man's death.

It's not too uncharitable to observe that initially, Erst was a man of slightly above average intellect, a tinkerer with the good fortune to invent a device with the power to expand his own brain physiology; indeed, he is widely referred to as history's first "self-made genius."

That this new capability gave him the wherewithal to revisit his early notes, which were generally quite sketchy, and buttress them by applying the most sophisticated mathematical models of his day (out of necessity and personal modesty, I've omitted such models from this retrospective), themselves above the heads of all but a few peers, roused not only the jealousy of Academy members, but actual cries of foul: gibes to the effect that the Multiverse Helmet III should have been awarded the Prize for its contributions, and not Erst.

In Erst's defense, this is circular reasoning. One may hardly blame him for putting his own invention to good practical use. Furthermore, most Erstian disciples were unable to come anywhere near his rate of predictive accuracy, suggesting no little input from the man himself.

It must be conceded, however, that Erst was very much a man of his time, whose radical ideas reflected a radical era. He later became a champion of the "Decentered" or "Thinkerless" approach to cognitive science that so pervaded academia in the late 1980s–early 1990s.

For just as Roland Barthes et al. questioned the traditional approach to a written text, finding the "author," for all intents and purposes, an unnecessary adjunct, Erst sought to challenge the long-held belief that all thought must be "thinker"-based—or even, necessarily, human.

THE IBIS

Like most others at the university, I couldn't remember ever exchanging more than an occasional word with Tim Stewart. Tim came and went, issued keys, responded to work orders within two days and emergency orders within two hours—but spoke to no one, essentially.

I'll admit that when his retirement party was announced, I took it as much as an opportunity to grab lunch and a slice of cake as to shake Tim's hand and wish him well. Probably for the small group of twenty-five or thirty colleagues who'd responded to the last-minute memo and gathered in the banquet room, including our new VP for University Ops, who'd come huffing from another meeting carrying a plaque, it was a little of both. We wanted to see a colleague off and form part of the polite company, but also to create a little break for ourselves in the midst of another long workday.

Tim had been compelled to retire from the Physical Plant due to an inoperable liver condition. His eyes were yellow and sad, his skin leathery from decades of outdoor exposure. But he managed a weak smile when Dottie Henderson took the microphone and started gabbing.

Dottie was an administrative assistant in the Registrar's Office who'd been at the school just as long as Tim, thirty-three years. She recalled Tim's wandering around with a hardhat during the heyday of the school's construction phase, always clambering up the scaffolding when a person was trying to talk to him, like a man who preferred the sky to the ground.

"Now he's grounded for life!" she quipped, making us all laugh.

No one stepped up to speak after Dottie, and the VP paused only a second before taking over the presentation and adding an anecdote of his own. He had recently misplaced an office key and called in the work order from the parking lot. Tim had been so diligent that a replacement key was already in the lock when he got back from lunch. I sensed this was an exaggeration, and Tim looked uncomfortable, too, probably since it wouldn't be proper protocol to leave a new key untended. But the VP didn't pause, segueing right into his script and thanking Tim for *Serving with Excellence* (our motto).

An awkward moment followed as the plaque was

handed over and photos taken. We wondered if Tim would make a speech.

He seemed to wrestle with himself a moment, but just said, "Thank you," giving the crowd a deferential nod. Then we all lined up to congratulate him, balancing our Styrofoam plates.

When my turn came, Tim extended a rough palm and we shook. I caught a glimpse of tattoos on the back of his forearm that surprised me.

One was a semi-circular wedge with other markings; the other a distinct Nautilus shell.

"Is that what I think it is?" I asked, pointing to the spiral tattoo. "Were you a Vert?"

Tim's eyes glittered for a moment, like a different person was struggling to look out of them.

"Tell you later."

***

The Verticists, or Verts, were a fringe 1960s student group seen spinning around campus quads, dancing like dervishes at concerts, or climbing up water towers for a dizzy high. Often mistaken for

American Sufis, they were nondenominational and "universalist" in a literal sense, believing that if the Earth were rotating at a fantastic speed, we should be able to feel it. Likewise, to cultivate a truer perspective, we must seek to regain our original, unsteady orientation. The tentative steps of toddlers, of sailors returning to shore, or of astronauts on the moon were considered exemplary of this sort of experience.

Yet in embracing the vertiginous, the Verts sought self-mastery. They shunned hallucinogenic drugs as unnatural, tending to impede an individual's return to cosmic harmony and balance. They tie-dyed spirals on their clothing, played a mean Frisbee, and became known as an active outdoor club with predilections for tree and rock climbing.

Tim came by my office later that day (he was a man of his word; "See you later" was his bond), and I offered him a chair.

I mentioned I was interested in the Verticists for an article on the roots of the World Pantheist Movement and would love to get his perspective, as there weren't many old-timers left.

When Tim didn't reply immediately, I asked him about the tattoos.

Obligingly, he displayed them: the characteristic blue Nautilus of the Verts; and next to it, an umbrella-shaped wedge raised over two forward slashes.

"I'm not familiar with that one."

Again Tim hesitated—but the ceremony of earlier that day, along with his illness and uncertain future, had stirred enough turmoil in the man to melt his usual reserve.

"It's the name of Thoth," he said, surprising me.

"The Egyptian god?"

"The god of equilibrium, charged with maintaining order in the universe."

Tim explained that club officers had added the tattoo as a totem of rank. This interested me even more, so I asked Tim if he would mind telling me about his group.

This time he didn't hesitate, only asking one thing of me in return: after hearing his story, I would drop any pretense of politeness and judge him as he deserved to be judged.

***

It was long ago, a much different era. But you already knew that. I was a sophomore at college—yes, I once was a capable student, though I never finished my degree—and I became attracted to the Verts for a number of reasons. It was only a small campus branch, headed by a young man named Wil and his girlfriend Cami. Wil was a tall, mild-mannered Nordic type, with Jesus hair and a little goatee. Cami was a real beauty—part American Indian.

I don't think our members ever numbered more than fifteen, and most weren't hardcore. None of the Verts were, at first. Wil was a lit student, and Cami changed her major all the time: English, cultural anthropology, religious studies.

Our gatherings featured peaceful activities like Frisbee football or "spin-ins" and DUPs on the campus lawn. I can see that you have a question; a DUP is a Dance of Universal Peace, of Sufi origin I believe—Cami's idea, naturally. Then a student named Swartt joined the club. He was a different breed—athletic, bristling with energy, always pushing things to the next level. He was from a wealthy background, a finance major, which makes me wonder what he saw in the group—it must've been the antithesis of the world he'd known.

As a rule, it's the newest convert who's the most gung ho: Swartt read to the group manifestos written by other Verticist cells across the country and tried to drum up a greater sense of solidarity. He's the one who guilt-tripped us into getting the tattoos—other branches had them, so he insisted we express our commitment that way, too.

Swartt had us climbing trees and flagpoles and anything else handy—you know, to induce that sense of dizziness and temporary disorientation the Verts craved. He'd had training as a rock climber, so naturally the group deferred to him.

It was inevitable that Swartt would join Wil and Cami as a club officer, but the three soon formed another kind of triangle. Swartt saw Wil as a rival for Cami and found a weakness to exploit: our club president, despite good-naturedly acquiescing to the climbing expeditions, was uncomfortable with heights. So he didn't exactly shine in those events, and grew more withdrawn as Swartt came to the fore.

Swartt, despite his aggressive proclivities, was not without his charm. He set out to win Cami over and may have succeeded. Like I said, it was a different era—we all spoke the language of "free love," not commitment, back then. I recall one concert Wil left because he perceived Cami and Swartt were sitting too close together. Icy silences followed at meetings for weeks, and the club came near to disbanding. But one day Wil and Cami showed up arm-in-arm, there were new members to initiate, and it was Swartt who sat on the outside in sullen silence.

I thought, at this point, he might abandon the group. It must have been painful to sit through gatherings of quasi-hippies and listen to far-flung conversations about Egyptian mythology and astrology without Cami as the prize.

But Swartt was only biding his time. Cami had raised the call for something "really, really spectacular" to celebrate the winter solstice, and a couple of the members suggested a road trip. Swartt had said nothing to that point in the meeting, but his eyes met Cami's and she asked him, point blank, if he had any contribution to make to the discussion as club treasurer.

What Swartt rolled out then was so unexpected it blew all the Verts away. In hindsight, it's easy to see how carefully he'd planned his presentation.

The first item he passed around was a photo of the giant statue of Christ the Redeemer on Corcovado

Mountain in Rio. The picture had been taken on a cloudy day and the statue's arms rose out of the mist like Hermes Trismegistus conjuring a spell. It received *oohs* and *aahs*.

Then Swartt passed around another photo, this one taken of the statue from a left rear angle, revealing Sugarloaf Mountain across the harbor and endless ocean in the distance.

"We're going to climb that," he said, pointing to Sugarloaf.

And he actually stood up, spreading his arms as though balancing on that faraway peak; and an image of striking beauty was burned into our imaginations, of twin mountains and two human figures facing each other with outstretched arms. Even before Swartt offered to take care of the flight details and financing himself, declaring that Rio was a climber's paradise he'd always wanted to visit and all we had to do was to say yes, we were in—thirteen Verts, all told.

***

The trip, as promised, was nothing short of spectacular: the first time most Verts had left the country or flown on a plane. And Swartt was at his best, corralling them at the airport and leading the march through security and customs with a swagger that made Cami smile. He'd insisted on a couple of trial climbs before we left, although nothing could prepare anyone for the sheer verticality of Sugarloaf.

He'd chosen the North Face of the mountain, leaving the choice of trail up to Wil and Cami. He'd casually tossed out the name of one classic route, known as the Contra-Pino, and a second, the Ibis, fully cognizant of the fact that the poetry in the latter name and club association with Thoth (the ibis-headed god) would make it irresistible. He reassured the Verts they needn't attempt the climb in one day but could bivouac overnight.

At first, all went well. Then four newer members took one look up the steep granite slabs and opted for a day at the beach—a desertion Swartt accepted with good grace, considering the cost to him of the trip. Two other Verts remained enthusiastic but lacked the arm strength to complete even the initial climb. Soon the expedition was seven.

Four others who'd made it as far as the first-day camp woke up so sore the next morning they elected to remain and take in the view from there.

Predictably, the three remaining climbers were Wil, Cami, and Swartt.

A long, slow, painstaking ascent began. Swartt led the way, naturally, pulling himself up by hand crimps to anchor the rope in the preset bolts in the rock; Wil held the belay for Cami, who climbed second.

When it came his turn, Wil did his best not to look down. And he was in fact a strong and limber young man, but you could tell he was battling severe nausea. He only persisted because of his commitment to the others.

At one point, despite being firmly tethered, he slipped back, banging his forehead and forearm against the rock and sending a shower of gneiss crystal below. When Wil regained his grip on the rope, Swartt and Cami could see he was bleeding.

Somehow they all managed to finish the climb, Swartt and Cami pulling Wil up the remaining feet. They removed his harness, bandaged his head, and applied a tourniquet to his arm. He'd lost much blood and certainly didn't need to look down to feel disoriented and dizzy.

Yet it was an inspiring sight—one of the most spectacular in the world. And so the leader of the

Verticists rose to his feet and limped over to the cliff, his gaze fixed unsteadily across the bay on the statue of Christ the Redeemer.

Wil stood a moment at the edge of the granite face and slowly raised his arms, trying to block out the pain. Then his wounds and acrophobia overcame him and he fainted. Unfortunately, his momentum carried him forward, and before Cami or Swartt could reach him, he toppled, unconscious, off the cliff.

The coda that followed was tragic and brief. Nothing could be done for Wil; that much was apparent from the sight of his broken body far below. But Cami refused to accept this, ignoring Swartt's warnings to step back.

In her mind, he wasn't sufficiently remorseful. She accused him of jealousy and of setting Wil up, which was probably half true: no doubt, Swartt had expected Wil to drop out of the climb with the others and imagined a different culmination, a shared triumph at the summit with her.

Desperately, Cami grabbed a rope and dangled an end over the cliff as low as she could manage—as if to wake Wil with it.

She screamed, "You're not helping!" when Swartt implored her to stop.

Afraid for her, he made the fatal mistake of grabbing at her arm and attempting to pull her back. Reflexively, Cami jerked away from him and lost her balance, too.

***

"She plunged to her death beside Wil," Tim Stewart added, bowing his head.

I offered him my condolences. Although by this time, I was more than a little puzzled by his intimate knowledge of events which had transpired on top of a mountain.

"Haven't you already figured it out, professor?" Tim spat, pointing contemptuously at the spiral tattoo on his arm. "This is my mark of Cain."

"I may have spent years at this university playing the part of a docile fool, but one lifetime of self-loathing and penance will never atone for what I did to those two good people."

A GLOSSARY OF LOST CULTS

Autotrophians sought to live close to as many plants as possible, fervent believers in the collateral benefits of photosynthesis. They were rumored to have been responsible for crop circles, early attempts to carve out living space on farmland. But the Cornfield Occupation was a short term strategy, an experiment in living "as a plant" before improved cloning technology became available. The group held that world hunger could be solved only when the flora-fauna barrier had been surmounted and human beings co-opted the ability to make their own food. Its predilection for cornfields was based on the immersive experience these afforded, and the presence of GMO seeds, thought to promote cell mutation. But the Occupation gave rise to a rash of tragic farm accidents that made national headlines, leading to a crackdown.

Bubble-Wand Theorists sought to replace String Theory, Superstring Theory, and Sir Roger Penrose's Twistor Theory with their own model. But they were undone by a shape that, while supported by quantum equations predicting stereographic projections of 3D spheres and orthotopes onto planes to form "circlets" and "handles," struck microphysicists as rather silly. To protest the lack of time allotted them at the 2011 Solvay Conference in Brussels, the group picked a moment just before President Jean-Marie Solvay sat down and Chair David Gross was introduced to rise from their seats, pull out soap bottles and wands, and proceed to fill the auditorium with bubbles. After a twenty-six minute interruption, order was restored.

Claustronauts sought to simulate conditions of space travel by spending extended "training periods" in phone booths, abandoned vehicles, and waste receptacles—the smaller the container, the greater the perceived act of endurance and derring-do. They wore hermetically sealed suits and oxygen tanks and took great offense if cited for trespassing or vagrancy, regarding themselves as serious astronauts-in-training.

Dark Umbrists believed that in order to explore deep space, human beings would need to acclimate to freezing temperatures and develop dark-adapted eyes. A cave was considered an ideal evolutionary incubator; but lacking access to one, the urban-based DU group did its best to subsist without electricity and central heat. The DUs objected to light pollution and made a particular point of switching off fixtures. This practice endeared them to office and apartment managers who appreciated the cost savings; however, when the DUs extended their repertoire to masking streetlights with black tape, they became a menace. Subsequently, they were rounded up and taken for questioning to police stations—where interrogations under painfully bright lights were enough to call them out of the shadows for good.

Grodornians (fr. Swedish for "frog") followed an active daily regimen of hopping in place. They were fond of trampolines and dancing the pogo. The theory behind this peculiar mode of locomotion had to do with evolutionary progress—a glib hope that over time, people might evolve wings—but of course, this supposition is thoroughly Lamarckian. It was thought to have been the M.I.T. Grodornian Student Club Noam Chomsky was ridiculing when he famously wrote, "saying apes can acquire language because they can learn some simple signs . . . is like saying humans can fly because they can jump."

Interferons were Luddites of the first order, worrying that radio broadcasts, TV telecasts, and telecommunications connections were bombarding the human body with toxic influences, scrambling brain waves and producing all sorts of ailments, real and imagined. They quite literally lost ground, moving from the cities to suburbs and then to rural areas, camping only where they could not receive a clear signal. Finally the Interferons vanished off the grid entirely. One cannot take seriously the urban legend that they founded cities under the sea, as saltwater is an excellent conductor.

Ionists were reactionaries who declared human experience the only measure of reality; that our senses provided us with all the data needed to navigate the world. Following the teachings of David Hume, who wrote that the atom, as a "least idea" of matter, must be perceptible to the senses (hence faintly visible, and even colored), Ionists claimed to be able to spot subatomic particles floating in the air. They favored old barns and structures which allowed chinks of light to bleed through, believing that in the beams were revealed "quarks" and "ions." But the sect's superstitions were roundly dismissed and its members accused of a thoroughgoing lack of perspective—of becoming enamored with dust motes.

Microcosmologists fabricated model universes for meditative purposes. Pebbles strewn on a dark glassy surface, droplets of water spritzed onto a photograph negative, or pinpricks punched into a black-tarp tipi to reflect stars of sunlight were useful in places one might not conveniently view the night sky. The Micros were fond of other simulacra as well: terrariums, snow globes, and ships-in-bottles. Too much the individualists to endure as a group, they grew lost in their own wee worlds.

Neo-Julianists took their name from a 16th-century resistance group which opposed the adoption of the Gregorian calendar. The historical Julianists protested the loss of ten days needed to make up for the extra time accumulated over the centuries and demanded these be "put back"; they were forcibly disbanded after a failed attempt to kidnap Aloysius Lilius, one of the chief proponents of the new system. Latter-day Julianists declared all clock time a misleading approximation, always a millisecond or two off, causing us to live falsely. They were notorious for acts of thuggery: liberating clappers from bells in church towers, or removing batteries from wall clocks in offices and classrooms.

Oozians sought to incubate themselves in the conditions out of which life rose; i.e., the primordial soup. They sought out bogs, swamps, and pig sties, sinking below the surface and breathing through a snorkel or straw. The moist ground was charged with a mild electric current—enough to invigorate, but not harm. The group theorized that lightning strikes had been frequent during primordial times but calibrated to the level of battery power by the mud. Here is where they believed works like *Frankenstein* erred: considered singly, a jolt of electricity is nothing more than a contrivance for restarting a stopped heart; to generate anything new, *prolonged* immersion in a charged environment is necessary. So too with creativity: a flash of insight is rare; most artists advance incrementally, through steady contemplation, more akin to Soto Buddhists than Rinzai. Perhaps it was inevitable that the Oozians would attract artists and creative types of all kinds, seen mucking about in mud baths at parties and mixers, spouting random lines of poetry or notes of dubious symphonies-to-be out of their blowpipes.

Quantametrics was a brief fad in Division AA football in 1970, associated with Head Coach Ernie "Pappa Hirt" Hirtzig of the Jacksonville Institute of Technology and his assistant coach, physicist Jacques Ondy. The concept melded a basic playground play—"Go out and get open"—with quantum theory (able to predict, with great accuracy, the location of particles). Ondy had observed the team's limited success that year was more often than not the result of receivers running broken routes and arriving to the ball by mere chance. With the recruiting lot fallen to him—receivers of limited physical gifts, but a quarterback, Sol Sukowski, who was an academic standout with a cannon arm—he argued that the quantametric approach was worth a try. Together, Hirtzig-Ondy drew up plays assigning receivers to "zones" rather than patterns, randomizing the attack and exploiting the man-to-man coverage of opponents. Thanks to hours of extra practice, Sukowski learned to predict his receivers' positions, or the speed at which they ran (though not, generally, both simultaneously). What derailed Tech's playoff run was the hasty co-evolution of defensive coverages. Bill Arnsparger of the NFL Dolphins, attending the AA playoffs in Miami, was said to have been inspired by the way rival teams faced down the Ondy-Hirtzig juggernaut. Sadly, the colorful Pappa Hirt passed away following a disappointing loss in the title game. It is rarely remembered today that his once-heralded zone offense led to the development of the zone defense.

Supersaturationists were perhaps the biggest thinkers who ever lived, taking as read the Big Bang Theory that the cosmos arose from an explosion of a super black hole which sucked in light until it could contain no more. But they reasoned that this light had to have been absorbed from a previous universe, and the light from that one absorbed from a still earlier universe; and so on, in an infinite regress. Not only this, but they argued who's to say our dark star wasn't just one of many, as plentiful as caviar in a beluga sturgeon's ovaries, each egg designed to produce fish to produce more eggs, and so on and so forth? Some suspected Supersaturationists of being rogue Creationists seeking to defeat well-established theories by pushing them past the brink of human comprehension. The group had a knack for lampoons of the eye-for-an-eye kind, making a 13.8 billion-year estimate for the age of the cosmos seem equally nonsensical as the six thousand year one: for on a scale of infinite time-space, the difference between any two finite numbers is negligible. They also aspired to make the idea of a "singularity" giving rise to a solo universe sound as exclusivist as that of a "deity" creating a single planetary system, hoping to frustrate further speculation and return more truth seekers to the fold. But their ideas were simply too vast in scope to be widely embraced or understood. Quite the contrary—Supersaturationists made the Big Bang seem, by comparison, rather homey.

Spacegrazers were an offshoot of older *Breathairian* and *Sungazer* sects, true believers in the benefits of absorbing sunrays directly through the eyes. Spacegrazers thought it was not only the sun that supplied nutrients, but other celestial bodies as well. Particular planets were thought to stimulate different systems: Mercury was said to have beneficial effects on the nerves while Venus fed the skin and Mars improved the heart and circulation. You could catch the Spacegrazers in parks lying out on blankets or lawn chairs, seeking cures for particular ailments or randomly sampling different planets like dim sum. But the practice was always intermittent due to inclement and seasonable weather. And restaurant owners lobbied officials to enforce laws against congregating in city parks after nightfall, perceiving the fad dieters were discouraging business.

THE MUSEUM OF HYPOTHETICAL PARTICLES: A SELF-GUIDED TOUR

You will find 3D glasses in a pouch in your museum bag along with sanitized headphones. When you are ready, please tune the headphones to Station 1 and press "Begin Tour."

Breathe deeply, for you are about to traverse a series of walkways and exhibition halls in which various energy fields will be agitated to reveal an infinitesimal universe, the world of "quantized excitations," or subatomic particles.

Electromagnetic fields will spark photons. Gauge fields will engender Gauginos. Higgs fields will give way to "the God particle." And you will see artists' renderings of previously undiscovered, only hypothetical particles.

***

Our first stop is the Gravity Center. You observe before you a twelve foot obsidian cone inverted on an obelisk base.

The sculpture seems to defy gravity in the manner of Barnett Newman's "Broken Obelisk"—one tip balanced upon another. Somewhere in that conjunction, we infer, exist particles of immense scaffolding power.

For this is the force that holds the universe together, the force that asserts itself despite the apparent absence of any quanta: massless, yet supporting mass.

As the lights dim, a tiny flash appears at the meeting of apexes. Like a geometer's point, it is only a hypothetical.

Did you catch it?

Watch again, and tiny dots multiply along the surface of the inverted cone, turning it white. It no longer seems to balance precariously but is anchored on all sides by a quantum field.

Now both shapes are illuminated; the center grows dark. Is this a black hole sucking in light?

As if in answer to our question, the light cones collapse—they were only a hologram—until nothing remains but a void.

***

The Inflaton Room is one of our most popular stops. It's filled, as you can see, like a children's ball pit, with colorful ellipsoids and spheroids resembling Jeff Koons balloon animals—of metal construction, yet so light-appearing you yearn to reach out and test their pliancy with your fingertip.

But stand back behind the yellow line on the floor and watch as the electromagnetic current switches on. The heavy balloons rise and drift apart from one another.

Laser lights fill the room like a security system gone haywire, buffeting the floating shapes on all sides, suggesting the presence of odd hypothetical particles known as Inflatons.

These are the particles that push things apart, the particles that caused the universe to expand following the Big Bang from marble-sized to the immense cosmos we barely comprehend.

Look again at those drifting, multicolored spheres: don't they, from your standpoint, suggest planets separating?

***

Kinetic Energy, the force that keeps us going. The floor begins to move now; we are standing on a motorized walkway leading towards a tunnel.

As we glide through the portal, the walls on either side of us, lined with old series photographs, come to life.

Olympian runners freeze at the starting line, then rise and burst to compete, reminding us that the impression of racing and movement is largely the product of our own perspective.

Next, images of rather sober-faced human subjects appear—still photos, though nonetheless bursting with potential energy, like Robert Longo's "Men in the Cities" work.

Strobe lights switch on, producing an illusion that the figures are, in fact, dancing.

As the lights cease their play, we observe the once-sharp photographic images dissolve into pixels, lit up for us to see. For all light is movement also.

What to call these pixels, these minute puzzle pieces of motion? Kineticons? Stranger things are known in the world of quantum physics. But it is time for us to de-board and enter Inertia Cave.

***

The motorized walkway deposits us near a sculpture

garden of stone people. It is a jolly gathering of contemporaries who at first glance seem to be our fellow tour-goers. Some wear headphones and appear frozen in contemplation.

The tour route marked for us compels us to intermingle, and the effect promises to be unsettling, like walking through a Gothic mansion primed for otherworldly denizens to emerge.

As we progress, we notice the stone people are draped in a fine netting of some sort, sewn on with a luminous, beaded thread. It increases in warp and weave as the figures lose muscle definition and distinguishing features, becoming more inert.

Look closely: they appear to be trapped in a kind of force field.

By now the statues are equal part humanoid and uncut stone, resembling Michelangelo's Prisoners; and prisoners they are—of Inertia. Our artists have suggested inertial particles in the beads of the web surrounding them.

Are you ready for the finale?

Mount a short flight of stairs at the far end of the room. When you are ready, hit the button on the plinth—brace yourself—the lights go down—we're in a dark cave.

Below us, the human figures have become a floor of glowing stalagmites.

Now push against the lit Exit hatch behind you and we shall proceed out into Main Hall.

***

Feel free to wander about in Main Hall: there is much to see.

You'll notice the lines on the floor marking the tour route have become magnetized, a randomized pattern of lines and curves. The grid crackles with interference like a Frank Stella etching and intermittently shifts thanks to computer imaging.

The effect can be slightly hypnotic; you may wish to sit down on a comfortable bench in the atrium. There you may view artists' renderings of the subatomic world on video.

The Garden of Exotic Hadrons adjoins the sitting area. In it, you'll notice shrubbery and rust-ridden sculptures resembling Richard Serra process art. But these are holographic images.

If you wish, you may get up from your bench and press a button to watch the holograms dissolve into sand and ash and finally into nothing—the operation of substance-chewing Entropons!

Don't fail to take in the unique Circular Rill which flows through the Hall. Thanks to the efforts of hard-working Rotons, its only direction is forever-downstream. We ask that you do not toss any coins in, however, for fear of an unforeseen butterfly effect.

Main Hall's vault ceiling is most impressive. It is raised to a geodesic dome and wind machines spin massive-scale mobiles of shapes resembling Clara von Zweigbergk's Themis creations, allowing anyone to observe the motions of everyday Spinons, Orbitons, and Holons.

Light shows are featured at 1:00, 3:00, and 5:00 under the dome and attended by mathematical visualization classes. Students sketch the increasingly complex Julia, Fatou, and Madelbrot patterns emerging from augmented Newtonian iteration values.

Children, too, may make drawings of their own imaginary particles, or "Imaginons," at the Exploration Station located near the gift shop, where they're certain to find souvenir glueballs and hedgehogs to treasure.

And why not stop for a Quantum Dog, Field Fries, and Fully Energizing Drink at the Quantum Café for only $8.99; half off on Wee Wednesdays.

We hope you have enjoyed this audio tour of the Museum of Hypothetical Particles! We ask that you place your 3D glasses in one of the recycle bins by the Exit and return your headphones to the desk for a refund of your $2 deposit. Please come again to see us and bring the whole family. Annual memberships are available starting at $79.

ANOTHER VERSION OF
PURGATORY

From Anders' *Guide to Travels in Europe*, First Edition, 1922, page 417:

At the Basilica di Santa Bona in Ravenna, do not fail to take in the cupola of Gaspare Gennari. It features one of few frescoes following the publication of Dante's *Divina Commedia* said to have adapted the poet's epic vision, particularly with respect to the Paradisio, which here takes the form of respectful *hommage*.

At the apex, we espy the Divine Rose; surrounding it, a majestically laid-out cosmos with spheres of heavenly bodies, recognizable saints, and innumerable winged cherubs. Toward the base of the dome we encounter a stylized version of the Purgatorio, one ring for each Deadly Sin. This section was once thought to represent the Inferno since the human figures illustrate vices but do not perform penitence; but instead, Hell is only suggested by a bottom band of flames in which contorted shadows of humanity are seen, but no identities may be discerned. Local bishops had debated whether any depiction of the damned could appear in a sanctuary of God, and to follow Dante's practice of allusion was not permitted.

From *Artists of the Italian Renaissance*: "Gaspare Gennari":

. . . the graceful embellishments of the [*Purgatorio*] mural are late Byzantine in style, harking back to Coppo di Marcovaldo, Pietro da Rimini, and Gennari's contemporary Andrea di Orcagna. Andrea's dry fresco *Hell* (@1350), which employed breded columns as a framing device, might well have served as an influence. Of further note in Gennari's painting is a mysterious figure repeated in each ring, which from surviving sketches and the Duomo self-portrait may be identified with the artist himself. Like Dante, Gennari placed himself imaginatively into his work, albeit precariously, for the impression one takes away is of a man struggling to avoid entrapment in a web of sin.

From L.C. Lewes, *Gaspare Gennari, Painter*, vol. 2:

Gennari's *Purgatorio* is much misunderstood. Its levels reprise the strata of Dante's mountain, yet the Deadly Sins are not presented in the same order: Dante's itinerary, from top down, is Lust, Gluttony, Greed, Sloth, Wrath, Envy, and Pride; Gennari's is Lust, Envy, Pride, Greed, Gluttony, Wrath, and Sloth. And while the circles are consecutive, they are not hierarchical, as if anticipating Hieronymus Bosch's later panel *The Seven Deadly Sins and the Last Four Things* (1485).

Moreover, the scroll pattern suggests several interconnections. In the Second Ring, for example, the artist figure regards a solitary woman, who in turn looks with envious yearning toward a contented-looking mother and child. A bold line connects this latter pair to the Third Ring, of the Proud, where they are joined by a husband and second child. Herein the two children, a boy and a girl, openly compete for their parents' affection, while the parents regard their offspring not with love, but as misers might regard riches; i.e., possessively.

Another curve connects this tableau to the circle below, where the children are recognized again, older and now appearing to vie for parental property such as might be bequeathed in a will; it is difficult, upon examining this detail, not to recall Niccolò Machiavelli's observation that human beings are sooner to forget the loss of a father than the loss of their patrimony.

Hundreds of scenes play out similarly, and it is clear Gennari wished to show the ineluctable nature of sin. The human forms are stylized, not intended as representations; nor restricted to one level, but repeated. There is an effort to depict sinners with not just one predominating vice, but many. It remains curious, however, that so few are depicted praying; and even these, in a context or with a countenance suggesting impure motives.

Further, as the eye travels ring to ring, there is no real sense of progress. The figures merely glut themselves on one sin, then move on to another. There is no escape from this Purgatory and perhaps more than a hint of heresy, because the only way for sinners to purge themselves of one vice is to have their fill of it. Throughout this mortal labyrinth wanders the Dantesque traveler, recognizably the interpolated figure of the painter himself, who gazes upon mankind's iniquities without judgment or emotion, but not, necessarily, without interest . . .

From "Gaspare Gennari and Clelia Manti: A Secret Love," *Journal of Renaissance Art* XIV:

Abstract

L.C. Lewes' interpretation of Gaspare Gennari's Purgatorio *is rightly considered a classic, but two of its suppositions must be revisited. First and foremost, the premise that the painter is the only distinguishable figure in the work. Facial recognition software has recently served to identify the Envious Woman (seen again in the Circle of the Lustful) as Gennari's mistress Clelia Manti. Was this a simple case of artist-model, or a deliberate depiction?*

Biographical evidence supports an argument for the latter, as a surviving letter of Gennari to Clelia references her desire for children. The evidence grows stronger when a second assumption of Lewes' is reexamined, viz., that Gennari only placed himself into the picture as an observer. In the Circle of the Envious, where Clelia Manti first appears, the pilgrim appears to look upon the scene with something approaching interest; and in the next and highest circle, Lasciviousness or Lust, we again recognize Clelia, an ecstatic expression on her face, in the embrace of a man with back turned. Nearby to this mysterious figure are coded references to the Gennari family crest. This was an indirect, though not unprecedented way for the artist to paint himself into his work and to suggest earthly love was not unworthy of commemoration, whether or not it dared "show its face" on a church ceiling.

From the Song "Clelia" by Samantha Gemm, Courtesy of Handsel Entertainment:

Clelia, Clelia
Your love was star-crossed
and for centuries lost,
but I regard you once more.

You passed unforgiven,
had to stay hidden from those
who would stone you
as a whore.

Clelia, Clelia
You watched children on the square
and whispered a prayer
one day you would give birth.

But Heaven in the sky
could never deny
the love which you touched
on this earth.

AN UNSPEAKABLE CONSPIRACY

The unpublished manuscript *An Unspeakable Conspiracy*, drafted by Stanton "Stan" Hill, my late colleague in the School of Arts and Sciences, was passed to me along with a ream of other papers when Stan died in a shuttle bus crash last May. Most of the pages were recycled, but I retained the MS out of curiosity. It had been Stan's "Kubla Khan": a work he'd represented to us as risky and brazen, yet potentially big. All I knew was that it had something to do with American history, Stan's field; and very likely with Abraham Lincoln, his passion. Stanton Hill was a descendant of Edwin Stanton, Lincoln's Secretary of War.

Following Lincoln's assassination, things had not gone well for Edwin Stanton, who was suspected of involvement in the plot. The tragedy inspired what would remain, for almost a century, the greatest conspiracy theory in our history—the belief that Vice President Andrew Johnson led a successful coup d'état. Allegedly, Johnson and John Wilkes Booth had been friends and sword-fellows back in Tennessee, sharing a pair of sisters as mistresses and seen gallivanting about together. They met again in

Nashville in February 1864. Most damning of all, seven hours before the assassination, Booth tried to check in with Johnson at the Kirkwood house. We know this because he left a note there which read, "Don't wish to disturb you. Are you at home?" Mary Todd Lincoln never doubted Johnson's connection with her husband's assassination, calling for congressional hearings. Partly to gratify her, these were held; but the nation had just suffered one shock and it wasn't clear it could survive a second. The Congressional Assassination Committee chose to exonerate the new president, leaving Secretary Stanton, who had been openly critical of Johnson, vulnerable to retribution. He was forcibly removed from his office by Federal troops.

***

We all readily recognize conspiracy theory elements like these, particularly in the age of the Internet, where the thesis of rumor blends with the antithesis of fact to become an unholy synthesis. To save you the trouble of googling: the Committee found that the disgruntled Southern conspirators originally intended to kidnap Lincoln, Johnson, and Secretary of State William H. Seward to exchange them for prisoners of war. On April 11th, at Booth's instigation, the plan changed to murder.

Despite a penchant for florid acting, John Wilkes Booth was at the core a crude racist—hardly the detail-oriented person to lead a strategic team. Not surprisingly, the other two assassination attempts fell short. Booth's would have failed also, had it not met with remarkably little resistance inside Ford's Theater.

I was expecting to encounter all this and more[1] in the Hill manuscript, along with a full exoneration of Edwin Stanton and confirmation of his suspicions, but what I found was something different. *The Unspeakable Conspiracy* was a book about dreams.

***

Lincoln's premonitions of his death have long been part of the popular canon. Stanton Hill's book begins with a dramatization of the most famous

---

1   For example, an alarming number of people on the side of justice where Lincoln's assassination is concerned "went mad" afterwards and were institutionalized: Major Rathbone, who tried to block Booth in the theatre box and received a knife wound; Boston Corbett, the officer who shot and wounded the assassin as he fled into a barn; and Mary Todd Lincoln herself, who never forsook her belief in Johnson's involvement in an assassination plot. Even for the nineteenth century, this is rather a high toll for the asylums. And manna for the conspiracy theorists, who speculate that all these persons might have suffered under the weight of some terrible realization.

of the nightmares. We follow Lincoln as he walks into the East Room, whence there is weeping. He sees a covered funeral bier surrounded by an armed guard and large crowd of mourners and asks who has died. A soldier replies, "The president. He was killed by an assassin."

From this account are typically drawn conclusions regarding nineteenth-century beliefs in mysticism and the occult.[2] But are dreams so literal? Hill would not have it so. He refers to a dream *fabula* as "a mute panoply of signs"—albeit its message, uploaded through the autonomic nervous system, may be quite visceral. He argues the East Room dream can be construed as a "warning" only if sent from Lincoln to himself (i.e., from his own unconscious mind). Perhaps a message that system failure was immanent and death would come soon—of natural causes.

Hill does not leave this chapter without making two further, crucial observations. First, several historical sources confirm Lincoln truly believed in the power of dreams to suggest ideas or conscious courses of action. Second, according to Ward Hill

---

2 Notwithstanding the fact that the dream *manifestly* alludes to an assassination, suggesting Lincoln might have picked up unconscious clues from the shady dealings of those around him and pieced the puzzle together in his sleep.

Lamon, Lincoln's old law partner, the President actually tried to *recant* part of this particular dream after he'd just recounted it to his wife and other witnesses. He changed the ending, claiming the body in the casket hadn't been his.

Why would Abraham Lincoln, or anyone else for that matter, disavow a dream? Here is Hill's gloss:

> In the act of turning his dream into oral history, a master raconteur like Lincoln could not have failed to recognize he had a good story on his hands, one of potentially mythic proportions. He may have decided to erase the climactic detail to spare his wife worry, or he may have had a sudden insight: perhaps this dream was sent by the powers above not to reveal what would happen, but *what his death might accomplish*. This insight is of the sort that emerges in the act of our relating a private situation to others and gives us pause to reflect. Lincoln would have felt a need to create a distraction for listeners in the form of a disclaimer, or to buy himself a little cover, like Hamlet, surrounded as he always was by a court of rivals, in which whispers and espionage were *intra muros*.

Even for a conspiracy theory, this is a wild cover-up indeed—the concealment of a dream! Stanton Hill was clearly working off of a post-Freudian model of slips and denials. But the dream revision is only the first of four major pivots on which his theory turns. Each has its own certain degree of improbability.

Pivot I: Lincoln came to regard his dream not as a divine warning, but as a divine directive.

Hill's baseline hypothesis is that Lincoln began unconsciously "working through" the idea of his own assassination[3] even as conspirators laid their plans. This is the reason he refers to the conspiracy as *unspeakable*: Lincoln's collusion with the assassins would have been primarily, perhaps exclusively, *psychological*, forming part of a "coterie of minds thinking as one."

Pivot II: Lincoln was aware that he was dying, and his primary frame of reference for thinking about death was religious and patriotic.

Dozens of modern theories have held that Lincoln suffered from a terminal illness, possibly colon or medullary thyroid cancer. Regarding the latter, Hill

---

3   According to a second source, Lincoln had the same dream on three consecutive nights, "which unquestionably would have led him to think past the naïve and superstitious view that it was sent as an omen." (Hill)

gives space to Dr. John G. Soto's diagnosis of MEN 2B, said to account for Lincoln's height, digestive problems, muscle and joint problems, facial features (thick eyelids, protuberant lips); and not least, his depression. Soto claims the president had less than a year to live, which may be an optimistic estimate. The salient point is, factoring in all we do know— Lincoln's dreams, self-awareness, and empathy for others' personal losses—he surely realized death was near.

Here, disappointingly, Stanton Hill's argument trails off into adjectives: Lincoln was "perceptive," "shrewd," "fatalistic," and "self-sacrificing." To him the fact of mortality was always most moving and most terrible. He'd known loss since an early age, from his mother Nancy Hanks and Anne Rutledge to those fallen heroes at Gettysburg and his son Willie. He'd invariably sought to put death into a purposive framework, finding lasting meaning in devotion to family and country, in virtue and noble sacrifice. To die in one's sleep was to die peacefully, but to die for the greater good, *pro patria*, was to die honorably and well.

Eyewitnesses reported marked departures in the president's demeanor and behavior on the fateful morning of April 14th. For some months Lincoln had resembled in countenance and mood a dying man, but on that day he awoke feeling cheerful. He described himself as "happy" to others and shared a dream he'd had of rushing over a body of water at great speed. Later, on his way out the door to the theater, he had inexplicably wished a guard "goodbye" instead of the usual "good night."

Pivot III: Lincoln's death was staged in a theater with a famous actor as assassin and unknown insider as director.

Stanton Hill's theory picks up the evidence of collusion between Booth and Johnson but paints Lincoln's successor as a hapless go-between and graceless philistine.[4] In other words, even if Johnson

---

4 The assassin assigned to Andrew Johnson, George Atzerodt, had taken a room above the VP at the Kirkwood. Allegedly, Atzerodt went down to the bar that evening to dialogue with the bartender, Michael Henry, and to ask him for a "character reference" of Johnson, which then caused him to change his mind. It is hard not to perceive Booth's own melodramatic sense of staging behind such a Falstaffian act of overreaching—to not only seek to brand an old friend with "innocence," but to have him walk away with a glowing endorsement besides. Booth's visit to the Kirkwood earlier that day might well have been made out of boastfulness; i.e., to drop hints something big was about to go down and he was at the center. One imagines Johnson, had he been in, receiving such information appreciatively, but obliviously. The Assassination Committee was likely right to exonerate him.

joined the troupe, it was beyond his talents to pen the plot.

The planning of the conspirators en route to Ford's Theater is well known, but what of any prearrangements made inside? What caused Ulysses Grant to change his mind about attending the performance that evening—was he dissuaded? How about Robert Lincoln, who would have been seated in the back of the theater box, blocking the entrance? What caused Lincoln's bodyguard John Parker to leave his post (this is a crucial detail), and was his arrival at the Six Star Saloon what tipped off Booth? Why did the assassin face such little resistance after leaping eleven feet from the box to the stage and declaiming the famous words of Marcus Junius Brutus: "*Sic sempur tyrannis!*"? How was he then able to limp with a broken fibula out the back door and onto his horse without being stopped?[5]

Like all conspiracy theorists, Hill is adept at weaving scattered details like the above into something resembling a pattern in order to "prove" the

---

5   Part of the answer is that the audience, in that moment of frozen time, could not have known the celebrity thespian, in making an entrance and reciting his line, was *not acting*. Booth's performance was carefully designed to blur the distinction between the theatrical and the real.

existence of an insider. Where perceived signs of choreography are found (not merely a string of unfortunate coincidences) there must be an invisible hand at work—or so Hill would have it. Booth was successful where his co-conspirators failed because so many "inside arrangements" lying beyond his control, such as the unexpected absence of Ulysses Grant's armed guards (who would have stopped him cold in his tracks) had already been "made in advance."

By this point, it's abundantly clear who Hill thinks the inside man must have been: Lincoln himself.

Pivot IV: Lincoln was complicit in the plot, understanding a sacrifice was necessary to unite the country emotionally and symbolically.

A weakness in Hill's theory concerns that word "complicit": does it suggest Lincoln (1) intuited the conspiracy plot, but nevertheless stoically acquiesced to his assassin at the last end (i.e., chose "not to resist evil"); or (2) actually enabled Booth by helping clear the theater box of impediments? Hill shamelessly equivocates between both senses, but it is obvious he thinks the bodyguard's departure (synced with Booth's entrance) is the smoking gun. He writes Lincoln was "a clever moral strategist" of a "deeply skeptical turn of mind" who "came to recognize the value of a noble lie." And he returns once more to Lincoln's prescient dream with its vision of mass mourners joined in sorrow, profoundly affected by a sudden and violent death—not a natural passage of life, but martyrdom.

Hill depicts Lincoln reflecting on *all those lost on the battlefield* who had been willing to take a bullet for the Union. And yet, though the War was won, the country still remained divided. Lincoln understood North and South would never join hands willingly but continue to hate each other like Cain and Abel without a common enemy or cause for passionate allegiance. Whereas his assassins were driven by short-sighted revenge, Lincoln would characteristically have seen past their ideological confusion and practical ineptitude to consider the long view: what was needed to sanctify and solemnize the peace was a suffering-together on the order of a religious sacrifice.

As it turned out, the crowds would be in the city that weekend celebrating en masse. The night the conspirators had chosen just happened to be Good Friday.

***

The mere suggestion Lincoln might have played any

role in a grand deception, even of the virtual kind, wounds and offends. *An Unspeakable Conspiracy*, unfortunately, has all the indelicacy of a first draft. Whether editors would have had the patience to nudge the MS towards a gentler argument we shall never know.

In assigning a truth probability to Stanton Hill's scenario, it's important to remember all conspiracy theories of its sort rest on a slippery slope. Even if the likelihood of Lincoln's regarding his dream as a directive rather than as a warning (Pivot I) is, say, 50-50, there are simply too many other turns.

Let us for the sake of discussion assume that the odds of Pivot 2 (Lincoln's awareness of his immanent death), Pivot 3 (the presence of an unseen facilitator inside the theater) and Pivot 4 (the identification of that person with Lincoln himself) are also about five-in-ten. These are generous suppositions stretching far beyond the bounds historian oddsmakers would accept, given each rests on many subconspiracy theories and fallacies. Even so, the chances of circumstances linking to form a chain must be smaller than the product of foreseeable outcomes, which is 0.5 x 0.5 x 0.5 x 0.5, or .0625 percent.

Less than a one percent chance of truth? Not worth the bother.

For this reason, and knowing full well no academic publisher would ever deign to touch such a book, I've done the next best thing I could think of to honor my former colleague's legacy: I've optioned *An Unspeakable Conspiracy* to a movie studio.

THE PLACE OF THE GODS

In his early travels to the tiny Cycladic island of Phyxos, ethnographer C.J. Wilson observed suppliants of all ages gathered to worship at the temple of the *thea*, or goddess. When questioned, however, natives declared the site to be sacred to all deities. Based on this newfound knowledge, Wilson speculated that the word *thea* must denote a site to "behold," or to supplicate oneself, to the divine principle. Mourning rituals witnessed on that first visit ranged from wailing and lamenting to stoical tributes spoken to the gods; from crawling on knees to hymns and processionals so orderly in the execution they approached the level of church services. This impression was borne out the following year when, upon returning to the island to systematize his findings regarding funerary rites, Wilson recognized a large number of natives unlucky enough to have been struck by personal tragedy in consecutive years; most curious, even after one factors in the relatively small population of the island. Even more astounding, while transcribing some of the natives' more emotionally charged and fanciful laments, Wilson found them identical to the last word to speeches he'd copied out the preceding year. Thus it fell out that a true etymology emerged: for these pilgrims weren't visiting the temple to pay tribute to the gods, nor to mourn their dead; but rather, to perform a play, for *thea* was their localized form of *theatron*, or theater.

SCHRÖDINGER'S DRACULA

Dracula is locked in a carbon steel coffin. Poised above his heart is a sharp stake. The stake will descend if, at the other end of the coffin, a Geiger counter detects any traces of decay from a cross placed near the Count's feet. The cross is forged of a uranium alloy exhibiting only minute traces of radioactivity. Whether it will measurably deteriorate over the course of the experiment, hence whether the vampire lives or dies, remains an open question. The fact that the Count was in a sense already both dead and undead ($\sim$ dead) upon interment allows us to safely put aside the discussion of decoherence, being consistent with the psi function for the system as a whole. Let us not forget, however, the critical role of the observer! If the coffin is first dragged out of a cellar into sunlight to allow for viewing, the wave function will collapse upon combustion of the corpus; if the moon is out, Dracula may once again walk the earth.

THE FREYA PARADOX

Order, as we perceive it, emerges out of chaos. But can a complex system ever revert to its initial, chaotic state? It would appear the answer is no. The chain of thermodynamic reactions known as the Arrow of Time is, by definition, *irreversible*—or so it was thought until the case of the former Saturn moon Freya.

The first images sent back of that satellite in the mid-1920s revealed polar ice caps and huge, crater-pocked landmasses. Sixty years later, a probe was sent. But before it could arrive, Freya had transformed into a primordial world of molten rock bereft of any recognizable features.

Understandably, interest in further missions dwindled. A Freya II probe was diverted en route to record an asteroid's passage in a nearby sector. It did fly close enough by the moon to send back more images, however. And strangely, this second set of photographs appeared to corroborate the earlier ones featuring ice caps, methane lakes, and protocontinents.

Scientists were baffled. The simplest explanation—

that the moon's orbit annually took it from one temperature extreme to another—didn't match the equations. Simply put, there was no known cause for Freya to have become superheated anew, as if devolving to its formative years.

Then a closer comparison of the two sets of pictures showed the contours of the polar caps weren't merely similar, but, for all purposes, *identical*. It was as if an ice cube had suddenly melted into a puddle and, without intervention of any outside agency, spontaneously refrozen into a congruent mass. Even more surprisingly, images of the continents, albeit low resolution, revealed boundaries that, when adjusted for the probe's angle, appeared to line up exactly with the early sketches—the same jagged mountain ranges and fault lines, the same methane lakes once thought to be candidates for supporting life.

This was theoretically impossible; it flew in the face of laws of non-equilibrium systems and thermodynamics—yet there were the matching attributes. Funding was reinstated for the original Freya mission, and enthusiasm restored.

Even as the Freya III probe approached the surface, however, it became clear we'd been misled again by this Jekyll-and-Hyde moon—the ice caps had melted; the continents were gone; the surface was now molten rock. The probe, upon landing, was instantly swallowed by lava.

Had the intervening images been relayed from an earlier space-time, like a movie projected in reverse? It no longer mattered. Further expenses could not be justified for exploring such a fickle world. Nor did the irony of the moon's having been named for a shape-shifting Norse goddess pass without notice from the press, until this joke grew old.

Sadly, Freya is thought to have been destroyed in a collision with the irregular moon Fenrir in June 2007. You're unlikely to find references to it online, nor to any similar cases of reverse entropy in books. It's as though the wayward moon continued to track back to its original formation out of gas and rock and beyond that point, utterly vanished.

If brought up today among astrophysicists, the "Freya Paradox" is whispered only as a cautionary tale, a reminder that so many of our apparent discoveries turn out to be reversals.

THREE DIFFICULT PHILOSOPHERS
EXPLAINED IN 100 WORDS
OR LESS

1. "I've attempted to come to grips with Plato's Theory of Forms in my work for years," the old classical philosopher says. "I've written whole volumes trying to elucidate them, but while I sometimes believe I am getting closer to understanding his models of ideal love, courage, education, etcetera, I of course never fully arrive there. I guess you could say, while I've found the concepts useful for my own work as templates, they seem to have only a kind of eidetic existence in themselves. What do you think?" he asks me. "I think that said it perfectly," I reply.

2. "It's just a tragic waste of a brilliant mind," my Descartian colleague's wife laments as she leads me into the intensive care unit. "Although he never succeeded in convincing anyone of the validity of *cogito ergo sum*. And now he never shall, I'm afraid," she adds, passing along to me the doctor's prognosis: following the stroke, the damage to the brain stem had been so severe that odds were nil of the patient ever regaining full consciousness. "Oh, he'll never

be himself again!" the distraught woman sobs, bending over the raised cot to kiss her husband on the forehead.

3. "You try to get employees to sign up for a free profit-sharing webinar, or even to take advantage of a company match," the CFO grumbles, "and I swear, it's like pulling teeth." It's the quarterly meeting of the Employee Benefits Committee, and my favorite kind: an "eating meeting." Fat slabs of roast beef and chicken cutlets glisten in their chafing dishes. "What do you all think? Do we have to summon the hairy ghost of Karl Marx just to get more employees on board with this?" Between bites, I reply: "He'd probably say, just try taking those benefits away."

THE BIGGEST MAN IN THE UNIVERSE

for Lakmal Siriwardana

"We're receiving some very strange transmissions lately from out on the magnetic highway," announced my friend Pushpak.

He spoke over the phone matter-of-factly, as though the magnetic highway was part of his daily commute and not the outer layer of the sun's heliosphere.

"Oh?" I replied. "Hello to you, too, Pushpak."

"Hello."

"So you are still on Voyager duty?"

"Yes, but these transmissions are different."

"What else could be sending back signals to the Deep Space Network, if not one of the Voyagers?"

"What, or who?"

"What?"

"No, it's a who. I think it's J.T.," Pushpak said.

"J.T. Waylon?"

"You always said, it's like that guy dropped off the edge of the earth."

"Wait! You mean he's not just playing around trying to mess up your transmissions? He's actually up there somewhere?"

"He's already passed Voyager 2 and 1. No doubt about it!"

"And what makes you think it's him?"

"Oh it's J.T. alright, no question."

"How do you know?"

"Because he's been asking for you."

***

J.T. Waylon had been one of my Caltech roommates in 1973. We lived in a quad along with Pushpak and another, very quiet Indian student named Iri. J.T. was a small, combustible sort of guy from Texas. He had wiry black curls he allowed to grow out a few extra inches in defiance of his father, a Marine officer.

Fall of our freshman year, I suggested we form an intramural flag football team along with some guys on our wing. Iri didn't care much for sports and took a rain check, Pushpak had never watched American football but was willing to try new things, but J.T. really went overboard and turned the games into serious business. He insisted on calling me "Coach," a habit that stuck with him later. We played five or six games, losing all but the last one, in which J.T. was clearly the star, rushing for three long touchdowns and actually spiking the ball when he scored.

We heard about that game from J.T. for a year afterwards. Then we all went our separate ways, Pushpak and I remaining roommates, J.T. and Iri moving into single apartments.

Despite his athletic pretensions, J.T. was a dead-serious, enthusiastic student. Whenever I bumped into him later, he was always in the middle of some new project.

Pushpak told me once that J.T. was becoming influenced by the Thecans, a radical campus group, but I assumed this would turn out to be another one of his temporary phases.

And then, after a couple of years, we never heard from J. T. Waylon again.

***

Theca Theory (@ 1971-1976) held that the heliosphere, the hypothetical outer layer of the solar system, acted not only as a magnetic field but as a time-space barrier as well. It was said to constrain inhabitants within a "solar realm," while by contrast, interstellar space was *diffuse*. Any object leaving the system was believed to enter a whole other dimension.

Theca theorists, or Thecans, were at the core skeptics. One of their tenets was that the cosmos really wasn't so vast after all. It only appeared so to our shrunken perspective. Once we exited the constraining influence of the heliosphere, our minds would expand along with everything else and become capable of greater perception and understanding. Clock time would be meaningless, as would distances measured in light "years."

The early Seventies was a psychedelic, turbulent time, so it seemed inevitable that this kind of thinking would cross over from astrophysics into the popular imagination to form a kind of liberation theology.

Thecans took their name from the outer sheath of a plant pollen sac, or insect pupa; the notion was that the heliosheath served as an incubator for the human spirit.

The Thecans were extremists, protesting that the government's entry into space threatened the integrity of an open frontier. They lobbied NASA to stop wasting taxpayer money running errands to the moon; to invest instead in technologies designed to free us all from the constraining influence of the sun.

Political commentators tended to write off the radicals as "Thecalistas," but the Thecans appealed to many well-heeled anti-government groups and paramilitary organizations, gaining some formidable friends before dropping out of sight.

***

"We think J.T. said, 'Made it past the Termination Shock . . . you wouldn't believe the turbulence of those solar winds!' Or something to that effect. The Thecans had access to Voyager technology and even spendier stuff, but those magnetic fields wreak havoc with transmissions."

Pushpak had never left Caltech, working at the Deep Space Operations Center (DSOC) in Pasadena, where we were sitting talking now. There were a couple of other interested parties in the conference room with us, too—military men.

"The second transmission, weeks later, was easier to reconstruct," Pushpak continued. "This time J.T. said, '. . . sailing across those bow winds like I'm riding Kon-Tiki. It's been thirty-five years, Coach, and supplies are low, but interstellar space is just ahead! Wa-hoo!'

"He's not kidding about those supplies," Pushpak added. "The Thecans were involved in the biosphere project and developed methods of cultivating plants and mycoproteins as sources of renewable oxygen and food, but J.T.'s craft can't be much larger than a motor home, or we would've spotted it long ago."

"I'm still trying to get my head around the idea that J.T., our J.T., has been the first human being to pass by all the planets, not to mention the Kuiper Belt, and has kept his mouth shut until now," I said. "Can he really have lasted in space for three-and-a-half decades?"

"Highly improbable, but it appears to be so."

If J.T. had a problem with the heliosphere keeping human beings contained, as did other Thecans, how claustrophobic must it have felt for him to be locked in a tiny ship crammed with supplies? How long could anyone last?

One of the military guys had his hand up now.

Pushpak nodded to him.

"Could he have been frozen in a state of suspended animation?"

"Not unless the Thecans had an advanced technology we don't. It's theoretically possible, yes. But J.T. was probably just trying to conserve as much power as possible for as long as possible and didn't wish to risk a transmission."

"That, or sending a man on a suicide mission might have seemed like bad PR to the Thecan group, which was striving to become more mainstream at the time," I speculated, knowing Pushpak wasn't really up on his American politics. "J.T. might've been under orders not to attempt communication until he was reasonably certain of achieving success."

"The boy's either a damn hero, or a damn fool. How does he ever expect to get back to Earth?"

Pushpak and I exchanged a glance.

***

"Does any of this make sense to you, Coach?"

It took me a few seconds to realize one of the military men was addressing me.

I winced at the name "Coach," but answered him in kind. "He's taking one for the team, sir. J. T. fervently believes just on the other side of the heliosheath something momentous will happen that will be to the benefit of all mankind to know."

"What sort of thing?"

"He thinks time will slow or stop and the perceiver will assume different proportions relative to the universe," said Pushpak.

"What's that?" said the other uniformed gentleman in the room.

"Passing into the interstellar medium might make you feel like a dry sponge suddenly thrown into water," Pushpak offered. "You expand."

"Or you are like a butterfly finally leaving a cocoon," I

added, falling back on the Thecan's favorite analogy. "To a caterpillar, a tree might define the entire world. But in becoming a butterfly, an organism crosses a threshold. Its new territory might span thousands of miles.

"It's not that J.T. Waylon expects to be able to fly, or to develop superpowers." I added hurriedly. "He just thinks he'll have a more expansive view of things, a clearer spiritual vision."

"And that's worth thirty-five years of solitary confinement?" snorted the officer.

***

"How close is he now?" the other man in the room asked.

"It's hard to say," Pushpak replied. "J.T. was nearing the edge of the magnetic highway when we last heard from him. That's the area where solar particles grow less energized and those in interstellar space begin to exert stronger influence. At the point the polarities shift, the magnetic highway ends and deep space begins—or so the Thecan group fervently believed."

Pushpak and I didn't tell the men the hypothesis that the heliosphere marked the edge of our system was problematic. J.T. was by now twelve billion miles away, but a thousand times further out was the Oort Cloud, a ring of ice and debris and planetesimals presently thought to mark the outer-outer limits of the sun's influence.

"Can we get a fix on him?"

"We have already done so. We are receiving a signal that is about twenty times greater than Voyager's, fortunately. But that still is about a billion times weaker than the one from your digital watch."

"Well, keep on it!"

"Copy that," said Pushpak, with just a hint of a smile.

"Because we intend to send him our own message, very shortly. Give us a couple of hours or so. We want to move on this whole thing very, very carefully."

***

"Well, that went well," I remarked.

"Could have been worse."

"Have *you* tried to contact J.T. yet?"

"We've sent several messages, and oh yes, I even signed off one from both of us: 'Congratulations, please keep us posted, Pushpak and Coach,' that chatty sort of thing. It takes seventeen days for our Voyager signals to reach the Earth; so of course, the kind of two-way communication these guys are expecting is never going to happen."

"It's possible J.T. has already reached the heliopause and the news just hasn't reached us yet?"

"Correct."

The two men came back in unexpectedly, demanding to know more details about J.T.'s investors, just who these Thecans were, any affiliation with the former Soviet Union, etc.

I told them the group had not garnered any headlines for three decades that I was aware of but mentioned names of a few prominent financiers and politicians with whom they'd once been affiliated. One just happened to be the recently retired Republican governor of Florida.

That got their attention. I felt reasonably sure, from this point forward, Pushpak and I would hear no further whispers about Commies.

Just for good measure, I tossed out the name of J.T. Waylon's father, who had been a Marine colonel back when I met him in 1973.

The men were out of their chairs even faster, leaving the room to make further calls.

"They forgot to say, 'Catch ya later,'" I said, after the conference door closed.

"Hush, professor," Pushpak scolded.

***

Three hours later, Pushpak and I were eating our Korean-Mexican take-out and I was beginning to wonder what my presence at the DSOC could possibly accomplish. Perhaps Pushpak had heard the word "cold" instead of "Coach?" He shook his head. Maybe J.T. had said he was flying coach class? Pushpak didn't even dignify that one with a reply.

Then I realized how harrowed my old friend was. He'd probably had little sleep since the first transmissions began.

After lunch, Pushpak gave me and the others a tour,

a tour I had been on before. In the control room, he played us back J. T.'s messages.

Creepy, to say the least. And with a strange remoteness that sounded mechanical and muffled, like a drone sending signals from a canyon.

At this point, we were waiting for the National Security Advisor to arrive as well as a "special guest," who I deduced might be J. T.'s father.

Pushpak was miserable, trying to steal a nap in his chair every time the two men stepped out, which was often. He wasn't the sort to enjoy a formal production of any kind and dreaded having to go over the story with each new cast of dignitaries.

But the fewer in on the discovery at this point, the better—and so I remained his only backup.

***

I hated to do it, but I shook Pushpak awake when I saw an elderly man being wheeled along the hallway outside the glass-walled office. The man was not in full uniform but wore a military dress coat over blue pajamas.

There were four stars on each of the shoulders.

I prodded Pushpak to lose his computer geek slouch and stand at attention.

"Greetings, General Waylon," I said, as J.T.'s father was wheeled through the door.

He looked up at me with a sharp gaze from under his turtle-lidded eyes.

"Who are these two?"

Pushpak introduced himself. He introduced me, too, making me wince when he said I taught physics for poets. He hastily added that both of us had been J.T.'s roommates in college.

The General was not pleased. "This hippie fiefdom was the worst thing that could have happened to my boy. I raised him to be disciplined, not to go chasing wild ideas."

We were shamed into silence by his tone more so than by any lingering guilt we could have felt over being part of some far-out conspiracy to blow J.T.'s mind.

"I understand you've received some messages from him lately?"

This time Pushpak's recitation was crisp and clear, and I was glad of it.

"What's that J.T. said again? Louder, boy, I'm hard of hearing."

"He said, 'It's been thirty-five years, Coach.'"

The General now looked a little distracted. "Yes, yes it has," he muttered.

***

J.T. was using Channel 18, the same channel and frequency as Voyager, knowing it would be readily picked up by the monitors at the DSOC. When Pushpak received a summons from his crew that the transmissions had resumed, we all excitedly headed off to the control room.

As we entered the room, it was quite startling to hear J.T.'s words being broadcast. I struggled to recall he was responding to an earlier message of Pushpak's.

TRANSMISSION: "You can't really mean Pushpak my old roommate, and you've brought Coach? Coach, I'm glad you're alive to see this." *End transmission.*

It took the full thirty seconds between messages

to explain to General Waylon and the officers that J.T.'s voice was not live.

TRANSMISSION: "I know I was a disappointment to you, Coach. But please know I've dedicated my life to serving humanity in one small way." *End transmission.*

I felt a very awkward silence all around me, until I noticed the General's eyes becoming watery. He mumbled something about little J.T. always begging to try out for his football team.

Then I understood. I bent down and whispered to the General, "I bet he always called you 'Coach,' didn't he?"

The old man nodded, suddenly looking forlorn in his pajamas.

***

TRANSMISSION: "The polarities have reversed! This time I know it's not just another bubble. I'm about to cross the goal line!" *End transmission.*

"I want to see my boy," the General said, very distinctly.

Some techs had been scrambling around us ever since we arrived.

"Why not, let's try," said Pushpak, speaking indirectly to his crew.

TRANSMISSION: "It does feel . . . different. Like a rope that's been holding you back your whole life going slack. Like you could . . ." [*transmission interrupted*].

"We were able to record the images from J.T.'s previous radio signals, so we can dial it back," said Pushpak, opening up another screen and positioning a cursor over a small blue oval.

"Light travels much faster than sound," he added, "so these latest messages from J.T. are arriving perhaps ten days after our last stored video."

We all stared fixedly at the blue oval, caught up in the illusion that J.T. was speaking to us directly.

***

TRANSMISSION: ". . . can't see anything out of this tiny screen now. Time to open the hatch and shed this metal shell of a . . ." [*transmission interrupted*].

"What does he think he's doing?" one of the officers snapped.

"That wasn't a hypothetical," the man repeated

when no one answered him.

I looked at General Waylon and said, more to him than to anyone else, "He's fulfilling his destiny. J.T. Waylon is the first human being to travel to interstellar space."

The General gave a little half smile.

FINAL TRANSMISSION: "Signing off, Coach. Been a long ride! We're all children of the sun, but ready to take a big step forward . . ."

End transmission.

We watched in silence, riveted to the dot on the screen which marked the locus of J.T.'s final words.

The blue dot hovered on the screen another second before it dimmed and disappeared.

And then we were seeing only a cosmic ocean of stars.

"My son was a great man," the General marveled.

THE RUNAWAY STAR

A Tale for Children

A medium-sized planet once found itself experiencing an energy crisis. Most of its oil and natural gas, plus much of its coal, had been used up. There were lines around the block at the service stations and you could see people sleeping in their cars overnight waiting for tanker trucks to come fill the pumps, just so they'd have enough fuel the next morning to drive to work or drop off their young children at school.

People had tried for many years to harness the power of the winds and ocean currents, along with the sun, but those alternative fuel sources weren't enough. If you wanted to heat a home or light a street at night to keep it safe from criminals, good luck. Scientists thought, *We need an energy source that won't get used up. Something powerful like the sun, only closer up. Something we can light that will stay lit for millions of years. Yes, that'd certainly help solve this unfortunate little energy crisis we've been having.*

So they set out to make their own star. First, they built a huge tank called a tokamak. The tokamak was designed to be filled with very rare gasses with names like deuterium and tritium. When electricity was shot inside, an energized cloud of mixed hydrogen-helium would form.

To keep the cloud pushed together, the scientists added powerful magnets. They knew that when the temperature in the tokamak tank grew hot enough—three hundred million degrees or so—the cloud would start to throw off sparks. Finally it'd catch fire and a tiny star would be born. It would be just like one of the ones in the sky, only small enough to keep bottled up inside its peaceful tokamak home.

When the reactor was ready, the scientists switched it on and watched the events unfold on a computer monitor. They wore 3D glasses so it was just like a movie. They clapped and cheered when they saw a gas cloud start to form onscreen, then waited as the interior temperature of the tokamak became hotter and hotter. At last, *foom*, the gas cloud lit up, and at the center was a glowing flame the size of a flashlight beam.

It was the tiniest star anyone had ever seen!

But stars, even miniature ones, are very powerful. So as the dot grew brighter, the energy produced by the reactor was strong enough to light up a whole city, then another city and another.

People were very excited. They knew they had a hard-working little star on their hands!

Soon, with the energy created by the star—which, by the way, was named A-1—topped off with all the energy from the wind, sun, and sea, the country finally had all the power it needed.

People were happy for many years. But as A-1 burned hotter, the sides of the tokamak tank, built of special tiles coated with tungsten metal, began to melt. Minute bits of used-up metal began to flake off like candle wax, and the surface underneath blackened and burned.

We'd better switch this thing off and replace those tiles, some of the scientists said. *You can't turn off a star,* others said. *It's not going to stop burning for ever and ever, remember? Then we'd better get out of here before that thing explodes!* So that is what they did.

Still, for a long time after, nothing happened. A-1 continued to shine and provide energy for the planet. The reactor had been dug in a deep pit, so people assumed if its core melted down, the explosion would be mostly underground. But no one truly knew what would occur.

Decades passed. Other renewable sources of energy had been discovered, so the crisis had passed and A-1's work was done. The scientists who created the little star retired and new ones took their places. Most of the young ones monitored the site from a safe distance and were not required to do much.

Then, one night, the whole planet shook! Trees fell over, and in the nearby cities, skyscrapers came crashing to the ground. Fortunately, no one was in them.

The scientists rubbed their eyes because they couldn't believe what they saw on their screens! The whole ground around the reactor was melting, becoming a cauldron of molten lava as A-1 sank into the ground. The little star was so hot that nothing could contain it, nothing cool it down. As it disappeared below, a bright ray of light shot up from the pit like a laser.

There was a huge hiss and steam rose from the pit as A-1 scorched the water table. And then more earthquakes as the runaway star descended toward the center of the planet, making its way through layers of crust one jolt at a time.

People worried the tiny fireball might score the whole planet with giant tunnels until it was completely hollowed out. Already, A-1 had almost eaten its way down to the core, where the temperature was thousands and thousands of degrees. Scientists hoped the little star might find a home there and finally stop burrowing its crazy holes. Maybe they'd still be able to use the thermal energy from the star, somehow?

But suddenly, there was another *foom!* as A-1 sped to the surface again, like a magnet that'd just met another magnet. And people watching at home on TV saw a glow rise from the pit like a hydrogen-helium filled balloon.

The cameras followed the runaway star as it rose up higher and slowly drifted southward, over the city, then across farm fields and forests, where it winked on and off, on and off above trees like a fairy light.

Finally, A-1 soared over the sea, which shone golden in the unusual night sun. Puzzled deep-sea creatures emerged from their caves with eyes blinking to see what all the fuss was about.

The runaway star continued to drift toward the tropics until it stopped and remained hovering, like a gentle nightlight, glinting yellow on the dark waves.

It still pulled upward, but the planet's gravity held on firmly to prevent it from escaping into space. And there the runaway star remains to this day, making nights less frightening and days extra-bright.

The island people came to name the star Aonani, which means *beautiful light,* or Aona for short. And they believe that if you row a boat out on a quiet night like this and catch a glimpse of her above, you'll be certain to have good luck.

THE BOX OF SPACE

A Tale for Children

Once a young boy whose mother was an astronaut was asked if he'd like her to bring him back anything from her next trip to the space station. She probably expected him to request a space helmet, astronaut autographs, or some food sticks and Tang. The boy thought quietly for a while, and when it came time to say goodbye, stood on tiptoes and whispered in her ear.

His mom looked surprised, but whispered back, "I'll see what I can do." Then a limo whisked her off to the rocket launch site.

All went well with the launch. During the mission, the boy stayed up late every night to tune in the news and see his mom float by on the cameras, blowing him a kiss and mouthing the words, "I love you, Milton!" (for that was his name). He got to Skype with her, although he didn't like that because her image was wobblier and her voice squeakier than the mother he knew. It certainly wasn't the same as talking across the room to her. And kind of weird, too, with millions of people watching.

When the day came for his mother to return to Earth, Milton was of course very excited to see her—and also to see if she'd remembered his present.

The limo pulled up outside the house and he saw a line of cars following behind it like a parade. They were full of well-wishers and reporters with notepads and camera-phones.

Milton didn't care if they took his picture or not. He burst out the door and down to the sidewalk, where his mother met him. They hugged and ignored all the flashes.

After a pause, Milton asked her, "Did you remember my present?"

And his mother teased him and replied, "Present, what present?"

But she pulled out a metal box the size of a lunchbox. The box was covered with reflective foil and sealed very tight.

"You remembered!" The little boy said.

One of the reporters leaned over and asked, "Whatchu got there, junior?"

And Milton answered him excitedly, "It's a box full of space!"

The reporter whistled.

That night, Milton slept with the Box of Space on his bed stand. It reflected the glow from his nightlight, winking like a satellite.

The next morning, he cradled the container under his arms and carried it downstairs, where his mother was sitting around the breakfast table with three of her scientist friends, chatting about her recent trip.

They all asked to see the Box of Space, passing it hand-to-hand and murmuring.

Dr. Rudolph was one of Milton's favorite guests. As he handled the box, Milton asked him why it wasn't floating.

"It's a heavy box," Dr. Rudolph answered. "Sturdy. But if your mother filled it in space, it'd be mostly empty, not filled with gas like a helium balloon. There wouldn't be enough air up there to fill a balloon."

"What happened to the air that was in the box when my mom filled it with space?"

"Ah—I guess it was displaced."

Dr. Vimal, seated to his right, had another answer. "Maybe the box was empty to begin with, like a vacuum," he suggested. "Then, if your mother went on a spacewalk and opened it, space would be sucked in."

"Not possible," said Dr. Humberg, the third scientist.

"Don't discourage the boy," said Dr. Vimal.

"Can I shine a light into the box to see what space looks like?" Milton asked.

"I'm afraid not, honey," said his mother, who was not only an astronaut but a scientist, too. "The light rays would penetrate the box, filling it with photons. Isn't that right, Dr. Rudolph?"

"Right," he said. "It'd be kind of like trying to spot your shadow on a cloudy day, only the opposite."

"Oh," said Milton. He picked up the box and shook it vigorously.

"Wouldn't do that either," said Dr. Rudolph. "You see, Milton, space is inert. It's not supposed to move, and if it contains any dust or particles, they're not supposed to move, either."

"Too late!" chimed in Dr. Humberg. "The Box of Space has returned to Earth and become trapped in its gravity field. Therefore the contents of the container are no longer part of the cosmos but belong to Earth space-time! Fools!"

"It's not nice to call names," said Milton, who reached for the box, placed it down on the table, and started to open it.

All of the scientists, even his mother, were surprised. But Milton had watched his mother out on spacewalks and had to see for himself, up close, what the universe was really like.

So he slowly raised the lid and there was a little popping sound as the seal was broken.

And then what everyone saw inside the Box of Space was: mostly nothing. Just a faint wisp of silvery glitter snaking up into the air.

Maybe a little cosmic dust in there after all, the scientists speculated. Dr. Humberg coughed sharply like he'd inhaled some of the dust or was afraid Milton had contaminated them with some unknown alien disease.

"Well, if there was truly anything in that box worth analyzing, it's gone now," Dr. Vimal observed, ruefully.

"Where's it gone?" Milton asked.

"It's dissipated into the air all around us," Dr. Rudolph replied.

Milton started loudly snorting air up his nose. "I-am-breathing-in-space-air!" he announced. "Aren't I, Mom? Aren't I?"

"Yes, dear," she said. "My little space piggy!"

WORMHOLE WARS

Wormhole Wars (SPEC Channel, Fridays at 9:00 EST)

Wormhole Wars is the latest cable offering in the oft-problematic Friday evening slot. The reality show centers on a recently discovered wormhole in Flippen, Georgia. A group of traders meets weekly to bid on items passing through the time portal. Viewers soon come to know their passions and quirks.

Quinn Denison is a biochemist specializing in unusual flora and fauna. She appears to have a bottomless closet full of Elie Tahari blazers, and one suspects she may be funded behind the scenes by a large biotech firm.

Her foil with respect to fashion (but possibly, some romantic interest there?) is Ronnie Graz, a flannel-clad local sage who purports to be interested only in salvaging used parts and scrap metal. Ronnie keeps a shotgun handy and exasperates Quinn with jokes about shooting strange critters that might exit the portal from another dimension. But his threat appears idle, for sci-fi flicks aside, no living creatures have ever passed intact through a wormhole. They tend to emerge as unrecognizable biomass—the kind of remains Ronnie disparages as roadkill.

Dr. Thomas A. McCloskey is a local historian interested in rescuing artifacts from the past, no matter the condition; which seems fortunate, considering his academic budget runs almost as thin as Ronnie's. The two have been known to team-bid on objects passing through the portal, particularly Civil War rifles and munitions.

Oren Dimino is the Armani-clad, high-profile trader primarily interested in items from the future. He is known for stepping forward and placing a pre-emptive bid on anything that smells like an investment opportunity. His erstwhile comrade-in-arms is a portly woman named Latrelle Owens, who has pretensions of becoming a high roller—but in fact she's willing to turn around virtually any small item for a profit. Oren sometimes uses her as a buyer, remaining on the sidelines while Latrelle seals the deal, particularly when a risky item stands an equal chance of turning out to be a zonk.

We learn that all five contestants have recently won a lottery for the right to be preferred bidders at the portal for one year. Like these people or not, we realize it's going to be up to them, in Season One, to navigate their way through past-and-future quandaries on behalf of the viewer.

In Episode One, "The Pink Foam," we visit each character's home base, starting with Ronnie's trailer, parked not far from the site where the wormhole was discovered on a local farm. The surrounding lot is a junkyard, but Ronnie proudly reveals two of his treasures: a sheet of unidentified metal alloy, which somehow got past Oren; and a Civil War-era dueling pistol, originally one of a set. Ronnie tells us Thomas owns the other; the pair had joined forces to outbid an exasperated Latrelle.

A shot of Thomas' office at nearby Gordon College follows to confirm that the companion piece has been mounted on a wall.

We next tour Quinn's refrigerated lab—where, under the aegis of the CDC, animal pelts are hung and tested, including strange bright yellow-and-black spotted specimens that don't look right for a deer or dog. Perhaps the remains of an extinct, or a yet-to-emerge species? In the background, we detect the presence of a secret greenhouse where plant spores removed from the fur are being cultivated. Beyond glass panels loom tantalizing silhouettes of lofty stalks and oddly curled fronds.

In comparison to Oren's fleet of warehouses, which

we drive past but don't enter, Latrelle's domain is homey, a thrift store loaded with odds and ends. She offers a glimpse of two treasures kept in a locked display case: a cat-sphinx dating to Precolumbian times and a souvenir figurine from Flippen, Georgia ("The Portal Place"). This is a cherub posed in front of a door, finger on lips, as if naughtily contemplating peeking behind it—in short, the kind of curio one picks up anywhere.

Momentarily, we wonder what the fascination is, until Latrelle shyly turns the figurine over to reveal the date: forty years in the future!

The main attraction, the time-space portal itself, has been gussied up with Fresnel lights, stone portico, a smoke machine, and a massive vault door. It looks like the Las Vegas version of an ancient shrine to Chronos. Behind the door is the sinkhole which mysteriously opened in the pasture one day.

A crowd has gathered behind an old wood fence to watch the day's events. They're warned not to climb up on it because it could break, and the entire area has been cordoned off to prevent crazies from running across the field and flinging themselves into the pit, hoping to travel to the future.

After Ronnie, Quinn, Oren, Thomas, and Latrelle gather their crews, we watch the vault slowly rolling open. This dramatic prologue is immediately interrupted with clips of interviews with the five and flash-forward glimpses of their surprised reactions to what they will see—very shortly—following the next commercial break.

Such teasers are standard TV fare, of course. But on this show, time fragmentation is, arguably, appropriate.

When we resume, we can tell it's been a slow day on the farm. Outtakes abound of contestant patience wearing thin. Oren spends most of his time on the phone and lobbies for shutting the portal down so he can depart without missing anything. Latrelle seconds him, naturally, stating she's remembered a hairdresser's appointment. Her words don't exactly ring with conviction (at this point and others, we're reminded none of these contestants is a professional actor). But the other bidders don't want to give up the hunt just yet.

And eventually, their patience (and the viewer's) is rewarded: from out of the mouth of the portal oozes thick pink foam.

A fungus? The renderings of an animal? Perhaps

some wayfarer who's fallen in? Those, at least, are Quinn's initial thoughts.

"Too much of the stuff," counters Ronnie, perhaps just to get her goat. "And besides," he adds, "it looks more like fiberglass. Probably someone is just usin' the hole as a shredder to discard some construction material or an old mattress. Saves litterin'."

Thomas seems quite taken with Quinn's hypothesis about human remains and speculates who this could have been, working his way down a list of Native American tribes and historical figures who had, at one time, passed through the area.

Oren is anxious to have the pink foam tested and tries to bribe Latrelle to cross the ropes and get closer so she can report back any noisome odors, or perhaps collect a sample.

Latrelle is having none of this—or is she slyly trying to drive her price up for breaking the line and risking disqualification from the day's bidding? She purports to be frightened of a whole bevy of alien creatures and refers to the pink foam as "space goo," only piquing Oren's interest further.

Meanwhile the sticky stuff has spread over an area of several yards. It plops, glops, and coils up on itself like climbing tubes at a kid's playground, and we anticipate Oren and Quinn are going to get caught up in a bidding war to end all bidding wars.

Are we dealing with biomass, or synthetic material of some valuable, unknown kind? Quinn and Oren briefly confer with their teams and then with invisible backers over the phone. Both openly rue the lack of available information. Ronnie isn't helping, raising his shotgun with a whoop and announcing if The Blob spreads any closer to those good people at the fence, he's going to start blasting away. They cheer.

Finally Latrelle ducks under the ropes to end the gridlock. She sidles up to the foam mound, pokes it with a stick, and harvests a cotton candy-sized swatch. Then she scampers back to the others like an ancient pilgrim returning with a wool-festooned branch from Delphi.

She's instantly disqualified, but not before she's waved her wand under the noses of Oren's experts, who confer briefly and reach a consensus about a "unique chemical smell."

Quinn, eavesdropping, now looks less resolute. Oren, taking his cue, steps forward to place a mighty, pre-emptive bid.

Another flurry of promos for the show follows as producers try to generate interest in next week's episode. We see the foam funneled into huge vats in a lab while chemists in safety glasses perform their tests. Company execs stride by with a glint in their eyes. Will there be an announcement to change the world?

Hard to tell, because we cut to Latrelle humming in her shop. She shakes her head and calls herself a bad girl, but then flashes a huge wad of bills and adds with a pleased smile, "Really bad."

Returning to the wormhole site, we see a downcast Quinn despairing that the foam might have proved a valuable medium for preserving specimens and Oren's invasive chemical tests may be destroying delicate life forms.

But of course, Ronnie is there to speak the reassuring last word, stating that he still thinks one of his neighbors was just making some trash disappear down a hole, and he wouldn't give anyone a penny for a truckload of the pink stuff, no sir he wouldn't.

THE ASTRONAUT DIET: A CLINICAL REPORT

PROLOGUE TO TREATMENT: Antigravity sessions were tendered to all study participants to inspire weightless imaging. Experiencing a "lightened self" briefly proved liberating, until the return to normal conditions and a public weigh-in had the desired effect of maximizing shame.

WEEK 1: Because a certain level of disgust with previous table habits is conducive to pursuing the diet with vigilance, subjects were fitted with airtight suits into which they naturally egested the remains of previous meals. This led to much discomfort and served to underscore the value of eating less.

WEEK 2: Transitioning to powdered drinks and food tablets may lead to a spike in glycemic indices. Stern countermeasures were therefore taken: (1) Liquid intake was curtailed to burn off excess water weight, and (2) subjects were spun in rotors to induce nausea, vomiting, and further excretions into spacesuits.

WEEK 3: A new regimen of fiber-laced, ill-tasting repasts established, water was reintroduced in generous servings to reconstitute dried foodstuffs and produce the feeling of fullness. Excess fluids ingested prior to simulated "space walks" made it harder for subjects to balance while performing before peers. (Wetting oneself was not uncommon.)

WEEK 4: Essentially the same nutritive protocol was followed, but with the addition of strained vegetables topped off with sizable doses of diuretics. Oxygen was "guzzled" through a mouthpiece before subjects spent time in a pressure chamber, causing stomachs and intestinal tracts to bloat uncomfortably.

WEEK 5: This week was the deep space simulation. Comas were induced in each subject to mimic suspended animation. Intravenous feeding was sustained to replace vital nutrients and essential minerals while reducing daily caloric intake to zero.

WEEK 6: Upon awakening, while yet drugged and disoriented, subjects were advised via hypnosis the simulations were real: they truly were trapped in space and the return to Earth compromised. The resulting fight-or-flight stress response to this perceived crisis, while damaging if sustained over time, proved an excellent means of burning off residual calories.

END OF TREATMENT: Informed the malfunction sequence had been a ruse and a splashdown was immanent, subjects might have been at risk of a binge celebration. But this announcement was followed by a dramatized sequence of a crash landing and *Survivor*-like sea journey on an emergency raft while waiting "rescue." Provisions were limited.

Andrew Agathon
Dr. Montgomery
English 101, Section 10
6 December 2044

Black Hole Drafting

Manned space missions to other planets may one day become possible through a theoretical procedure known as Black Hole Drafting (BHD). BHD involves taking up a strategic position near a black hole and then observing, via satellite, space station, or other spacecraft, the asteroids and planetoids pulled into its gravitational field ("Breakthrough"). It may serve as an alternative to longer-term space exploration by closing the distance between Earth and interstellar objects millions of light-years away. During a recent panel discussion aired on CNN, Dr. Iri K. Namboothiri of NASA raised the following challenge: "Why should we force our way through space with rocket thrusters, trying to reach distant solar systems and galaxies, if we can let the universe come to us?" (qtd. in "Breakthrough").

The problem of an ever-expanding universe has long discouraged space travel outside of our own solar system. According to Dr. David L. Balder, Regents' Professor of Astronomy at the University of Arizona, the Big Bang is to blame for a paradox: if other systems are moving away from us at the speed of the light, our technology never really has a chance to catch up. He compares this to trying to hit a moving target while still designing the weapon (Balder). And whereas some scientists theorize that the universe might expand and collapse in repeated cycles, or *kalpa*, waiting billions of years for stellar objects to approach us in the next Great Contraction postpones the idea of space travel indefinitely, well past the point in time our own sun will be able to support life (Mayat).

What we now better understand, however, is that the universe is simultaneously expanding and contracting in different sectors all the time. Recent computer-generated "contour maps" of interstellar space have revealed convolutions resembling the fronts on a weather map, or pleats on a curtain (Dash). According to many astrophysicists, black holes are places where the fabric of the cosmos is actively trying to "knit itself together" following the Big Bang. Black holes pull the curtain tighter, giving the universe greater integrity and uniformity. In this respect, they function much more like the strong force which holds the nucleus of an atom together than the weak force which leads to decay (Dash).

Black holes have gotten a bad rap as "planet-and-sun swallowers" ("Breakthrough"). This is true of some, but not all. Small holes are more common, working like robotic vacuum cleaners, eating their fill and stopping. Several of these smaller black holes (Balder calls them "utilitarian" holes) have been discovered in interstellar space and are revolutionizing our understanding of the cosmos. Where we once had to postulate the existence of galactic magnetic fields or interstellar winds to explain unexpected variances in data, we now recognize places where the time-space fabric is being warped due to local gravity associated with utilitarian black holes (Balder).

Recently, a mid-sized black hole named Tantis 12 was discovered outside the Kuiper Belt. This hole is busily pulling in asteroids and planetoids as big as the former Pluto (Okpish). Several NASA scientists have hailed this as a golden opportunity to put BHD to the test and observe a parade of interstellar objects—perhaps even to go "dwarf planet hopping" as T-12 becomes neutrino-satiated and starts trawling for objects at a much slower speed (Okpish). Backers of a proposed Tantis 12 mission argue it could become a trial run for reconnaissance missions to other, larger black holes ("Breakthrough"), which warp time-space so powerfully they create huge convolutions and pull entire planetary systems nearer.

Black Hole Drafting is not without its critics, of course. Before a manned mission to Tantis 12 is ever attempted, NASA scientists must learn more about the extent of the "safe zone" lying outside a black hole's gravitational cone (Balder). This will require a closer study of the trajectories of the asteroids and planetoids T-12 currently consumes and perhaps even some selective "seeding" of the hole with no-longer-functioning satellites or jettisoned space junk (Dash).

To conclude, although universe expansion was once thought to rule out travel to other planets, outstripping our technological advances, the contraction folds created by black holes may be drawing sectors of the cosmos close enough for us to visit. One day in the not-too-distant future, Black Hole Drafting could allow human beings to explore alien worlds as they are pulled from their orbits, ushering in a whole new era of space exploration.

Word Count: 750

Note to Dr. Montgomery: This is only a first draft, no Works Cited yet.

RETHINKING THE DON

First Broadcast on NPR's This Cosmic Realm
Sunday, May 8, 2704

2620: that now forgettable year when we first attempted to settle on another planet. The site of our cosmic Jamestown was originally known as Kepler 186-f; and later, after the naming rights to planets had been fully monetized, by several other designations. The longer lasting of these being Planet Helu-Nano, Planet Baotech, Planet Qatarion, PlanDisney, Planet Häagenquark, and Planet Putneft. The clever market watchers at Putneft Hydrofracking had postponed their naming bid until the eve of the 2600 International Stellar Convention.

From the start, there was buyer's remorse. We'd already had some cause to wonder about the supposedly superintelligent inhabitants of our sister planet based on received transmissions that weren't wholly gibberish, but not exactly coherent, either. We'd always given the Putneftians the benefit of the doubt, imagining they must be a refined, mystical race to dash off such elliptical replies to our overtures of friendship, perhaps too busy communing with higher-level tasks to interface with us.

As it drew nearer to the end of its six-hundred year mission, however, the twenty-fourth generation crew of the Floating Embassy of the World (the FEW) grew increasingly apprehensive. It renewed longstanding requests for pictures, documents, samples of music and art—anything at all that might ease the imminent assimilation into an unknown world. The ship transmitted images of Earth artifacts, hoping to prompt the Putneftians to answer in kind.

What the natives beamed back were messages which seemed to mimic those the FEW had sent, badly out-of-focus photos that looked like faint attempts to copy humankind's own, and music which was just . . . noise.

The FEW felt obliged to refrain from further cultural exchanges when its legal team warned these might compromise the Doctrine of Noninterference (the DON). Inhabitants of our sister planet might get the wrong idea about the mission, regarding the mostly scientist crew as hostile colonizers.

***

From the partially preserved *Captain's Log of Ezerrah Tomm*, recently discovered by officials of the Anarticon Corporation following its hostile takeover of Putneft Hydrofracking:

". . . small, yellow complected, rather childlike in appearance, with wide, duckbilled grins and forelocks that fell over their faces, giving them a cross-eyed appearance. Despite a surface temperature of zero degrees, the Indigens were unclothed, exposing a wisp of hair covering paired genitalia of both sexes. It was evidently mating season, for they were face-to-face bonding, searching out counterparts with reverse-aligned members. When our landing party stepped out to greet them, they attempted to pull off our suits and helmets; from an atmospheric standpoint, these had been unnecessary, but now proved useful as protective gear."

Comment: listeners with small children might wish to mute this next portion of the story.

"The Indigens then set to vigorously humping our legs. Unsure whether this was a customary greeting or a frenzied carryover from the mating season, we allowed the sordid ritual to continue to its end, although this was the first of several incidents which gave rise to the reflection that the Doctrine of Noninterference might be in need of some adjustment.

"A second such occurrence ensued when two of the natives upended our Chief Cultural Officer, a petite woman. Whereupon I interposed myself between parties, helping the officer back to her feet while gently but firmly remonstrating with her enthusiastic welcomers."

Comment: It is clear from the entries retrieved from his log that Captain Tomm, like others aboard the FEW, had sustained himself over the course of history's longest recorded space voyage on antiquarian novels from the Infinite Library.

"At this point, as captain, I attempted to engage the crowd in conversation. With the aid of our linguists, I'd prepared a short speech utilizing every known word of their tongue; or rather, what could be interpolated of it based on the entire database of our species' communication. I found it impossible to gain their attention, however, without first firing a shot in the air; risking, as I did so, the appearance of aggression.

"The shot succeeded in getting nearby Indigens to detach from one another and stand at awed attention, but they soon began grabbing at my gun out of idle curiosity. I cut the speech short, for they weren't listening—only repeating phrases of my own.

"This led to a subsequent reexamination of our assumptions about their language—in particular, whether over past decades when the FEW had received snatches of communication, what was heard were only echoes of its own transmissions, perhaps resulting from magnetic disturbances in the atmosphere—muted echoes of our greetings, short bursts resounding like replies in the affirmative to our queries. This hypothesis was later confirmed when it became clear that the natives had no spoken or written language at all . . .

"By this point, the crowd was massed outside the ship and more Indigens were vying for my gun (their hands were much like ours, tiny, yet with opposable thumbs). I felt it necessary to call the tiny landing party back to the FEW."

***

Comment: Behind Captain Tomm's thinly veiled disappointment in the Putneftians was no doubt the recent history of the FEW, the collapse of the Seven Generations and the Pure One.

The original crew of 128 had been selected not merely on the basis of individual merit and willingness to sacrifice for future generations, but upon its genetic diversity. A strict program of arranged marriages was laid out to sustain this balance.

The plan had been followed religiously during the mission's first two hundred years, yielding seven generations and a Pure One: a genetic singularity who in turn was to breed with sixth-removed relatives to produce patriarchs of new family trees. But the Pure One turned out to be infertile, and the hasty intermarriages to follow only sought to unite as many fourth- and fifth-removed cousins as possible.

This backup plan proved difficult to sustain. Home TV viewers watching relationships unfold aboard the FEW lobbied for love unions over eugenics, encouraging many first-cousin marriages during the FEW's quadricentennial celebration. From then on, in each generation the inbreeding only grew worse.

By the six-hundred year mark, few fully functioning crew members were left—twelve, not counting androids. In the hold were kept two hundred offspring incapable of contributing to the vessel's operation; indeed, unable to look after themselves.

From back on Earth came dark whispers of jettisoning the cargo in deep space so as not to make the wrong impression on our future hosts, who might mistake the FEW for a hospital ship.

Optimists held out hope that with their superior intelligence, the Putneftians might offer some hope of treatment.

***

Captain Ezerrah Tomm's log continues. Again, listeners are warned some material may be unsuitable for young children:

". . . fond of low-hanging fruit they called *berqua*, which tasted of sour milk and produced painful belching among our crew. The Indigens competed for this fruit and ate plentifully of insects resembling scarabs. They drank at the same waterholes whereat they swam and were oblivious to matters of hygiene, actually defecating while walking, like horses. A cholera-like illness ran rampant among them, killing as many as 4 of 5.

"Again it proved difficult to refrain from violating the DON in this matter, viz., to teach the natives something about health. But as my Science Officer Mr. Cogz rightly cautioned, the resulting overpopulation of Putneftians might overwhelm the ecosystem, wiping out both insects and foul-tasting fruit.

"Meantime the crew did its level best to keep the masses in our ship's hold fed on dwindling supplies, supplementing these with servings of *berqua*, but protests below decks to this dietary innovation were violent, resulting in one provisions officer nearly being stoned to death with pits. It also proved impossible to sanitize the fruit without clean water, with the result that an infectious mania spread among the Innocents, characterized by hyperactivity, impulsive behavior, tearing off of clothes, and commencement of Putneftian-style orgies."

***

You're listening to *This Cosmic Realm,* and I'm your host, Riz Lanwell. Our program today is titled "Rethinking the DON."

In this first act, we've been reviewing the mission to Anarticon, formerly known as Planet Putneft, of that hardy crew of scientists and colonists who were part of the Floating Embassy of the World, the FEW. It was believed until recently the ship had crashlanded and all would-be colonists were wiped out, but the recently discovered *Captain's Log of Ezerrah Tomm* has caused us to radically rethink that notion . . . and as we do so, to "rethink the DON."

Let's pick up Captain Tomm's narrative a little later, just as the situation with the Putneftians threatens to get out of hand:

". . . our security team escorted representative Indigens two at a time into the ship as a diplomatic gesture—but predictably, it became a challenge to maintain order.

"We displayed images of the planet taken from space and pointed outside, but they only wished to toggle control knobs, stretch and distort the screen picture, and snort. In so doing they discharged a black, sticky substance which seemed potentially virulent and kept maintenance bots busy mopping—a circumstance they found most entertaining. And there may have been some silent communication among them afterwards, because the next visiting pair picked its moment to pull a ruse: one urinating and tying up the bots while the other broke for the ship's guns, turning these upon a group of outside onlookers and vaporizing them before any of us could intervene.

"These Indigens appear to set no great store on life, perhaps due to their own high mortality rate, nor to follow any ethical code. I found it difficult to hold fast to the DON when the same one who'd just killed his fellows looked over to me with his duckbilled grin and tapped the palm of one hand with the index finger of the other in that universal gesture signifying "more.""

"I felt like taking the little devil over my knee and giving him a sound thrashing instead. But once again I reminded myself: *Doctrine of Noninterference, Doctrine of Noninterference.*"

***

Comment: All Captain Tomm's further attempts to create a bond with the Putneftians by inviting them into his "home" similarly backfire. Very soon the situation spirals completely out of his control:

". . . gave the order to Mr. Cogz to permanently disable the ship's arsenal; knowing, even as I did so, I might live to regret my decision. Sooner or later we must open the hatch for air and the waiting Indigens could rush us in a body and seize control. We might hold them off, at great cost of life, but that level of disruption to their self-sufficient little world was surely unjustifiable, and hardly consistent with the FEW's original mission of spreading goodwill to inhabitants of our sister planet.

"The higher course was to detonate the ship and declare the mission over. Yet I could not in conscience do so with the Innocents in the hold; those in whom the sins of the fathers and mothers had borne such helplessness."

Comment: There's a great deal of damage here to Captain Tomm's log, retrieved during the next mission from the severed head of android Science Officer Mr. Cogz, found buried in a refuse pit.

What we can infer from fragmentary entries is that the dozen functioning crew members held off hostile attacks of the Putneftians for some months until the only surviving members of the FEW were Captain Tomm himself and the two hundred-or-so members in the hold:

". . . pinned in now on *both* sides. The Indigens callously trample one another while pounding against the ship with enough force to rock it. From below deck come thuds and muffled shouts of hungry and frightened Innocents; all of them, with one voice, begging for release . . .

". . . therefore I am obliged to issue final orders to my faithful science officer as Captain of the FEW . . ."

Comment: Captain Tomm's final orders were twofold. The second one, clearly, was to open the hatch to the ship's hold. The first order is a little garbled, but you can just hear it above the background noise:

". . . Fire when you are ready, Mr. Cogzs . . ."

Comment: And so the much-tormented Captain Ezerrah Tomm chose to go down with his ship.

**

We can only imagine the scene that unfolded next.

Consider: From below emerges a group of would-be colonists. They roam the ship searching anxiously for their caretakers, encountering no one except the faithful Mr. Cogzs, who does his best to coach them throughout the waning hours of the night and on into the next morning, when the Putneftians will be at their most dormant.

Morning arrives. The doors of the ship open.

As they step out under the light of a just-rising red sun, the new colonists take a first-ever look at the natural world.

It must be lonely in that initial moment on an alien planet—until a corresponding group of Putneftians approaches.

The diminutive people rub their cross-eyed countenances to fend off sleep. It is the first good look any of them have gotten at humanity en masse, minus the spacesuits and weaponry.

No doubt, the two groups stand gazing at each other for a long, long time. And then they do what the original crew, with all its technological know-how, never thought to do: they embrace.

***

Epilogue: We hadn't heard until recently about the Lost Colony of Planet Putneft. But we learn the rest in school. The next ship of settlers, on their storied ship the Lightracer, made landing on the planet seventy-six years later, a wormhole shortcut slicing a whopping 525 years off the trip.

There the crew would meet the most beautiful race imaginable, orange-lemon skinned beings who danced away most days under the pleasant warmth of a red sun.

The Anarticans were only slightly undersized by our standards, hardly the pygmies of Tomm's account; and modest of manner, with shining eyes and a neat tuft of hair atop their heads.

They lived in stone abodes, cultivated familiar-looking vegetables to supplement their fruit diet, and got along quite peaceably with one another. Most wonderfully, they were able to communicate to ambassadors in Standard Interstellar English, validating a long-held belief that the planet harbored a race of surpassing intelligence.

When queried about a previous expedition, Anarticans shook their heads. Eventually they would share a fabulous myth of a gentle people who'd descended from the stars to found their civilization, and to whom all could trace their roots.

Unfortunately, having no real concept of time, they could only repeat that this had been long, long ago, before any of them had been born.

RETRACING MY STEPS

I decided to avail myself of that dream ability to discover things. You know how sometimes when you misplace an object, you decide to "sleep on it" to see if the location comes back to you? I'd been puzzling over numbers and bills that evening, so in my sleep set out on a virtual dream-tour of the house to locate a missing pocket calculator. Instantly all sorts of hidden corners came into view, actually turning light blue in the darkness, as if perceived through night-vision goggles. There was the edge of my desk where it slid into space; there the mountainous steppes of a bookcase, rising beyond reach. There the void of the wastebasket, a simple enigma. I attempted the kitchen drawer, a dangerous ghetto of crisscrossed utensils—nothing. I tried probing beneath the rainforest fronds of potted plants, slid my fingers into unseen earth—again nothing. I puzzled over the quandary of whether to turn on a nearby lamp: if I put an end to the darkness, would I lose my ability to discover lost items? Or would it make no difference, as the lamp was also in the dream? I resolved not to take such a risk, but then grew apprehensive I might have been sleepwalking all this time, a cruder questing than I'd hoped for or imagined. I set out on a trek across the rough carpet, through the narrow pass of the hallway. Now I was retracing my last steps before bed, a cold trail from a half-life blocked to me. Reflexively my hand drifted to my pillow, from which I derived comfort: since I remained prone, hadn't I succeeded in preserving a quantum of consciousness without breaking the spell of sleep? Yet this thrill of attainment proved my undoing. When I tried to refocus my thoughts on the lost object, I couldn't—not from any lack of resolve, mind you—but because I'd recalled I did not own a pocket calculator.

DREAM METAPHORS

I. Going Off-Road / Sidewinding

In some of my dreams, a detour will appear off the interstate. This usually becomes a welcome, forested trail. Darker dreams might terminate in impassable rocks or mud, and an underlying regret for seeking to break the monotony of my commute.

Tonight I veer off onto the shoulder to pick up one such trail. The land is flat and dry. I am passed by dozens of people joining a Walk Across America headed the opposite way.

After the walkers pass, I spot a mysterious dog in the distance. It is sleek and black with gray markings and winds side-to-side. As it comes closer, I see this mute creature has no facial features and no fur—a serpent.

In our sleep, we are all similarly sidewinders.

II. Parallel Universe / Faulty Parallel

Working again at a bank, I'm surprised to find I've attracted the notice of two female employees. *I must be looking OK for my age*, I reflect. Then I realize I'm no longer my chronological self; this must be a parallel career in another possible past.

To be me, of course, I must still retain an older consciousness, yet be familiar enough with my surroundings to function. Fortunately, as I exit the facility, I recognize one of my old cars in the parking lot so I know just where to go.

As I pull out of my spot, however, I go into a skid and have to spin the car back into place, barely missing another vehicle.

III. Getaway Car / Getting Carried Away

My teenage friends and I have rebuilt an old car. The auspices of this project are vaguely criminal—we plan to use it to escape our parents.

The car is a luxury vehicle from the 1940s—steel frame, wood side panels. One friend and I put on the finishing touches while the others await us at a nearby waterfront.

When we arrive, they hop in. The consensus is to motor out across the water. So we putter down a channel leading to an open harbor, but soon the vehicle starts to leak. Kneeling on the bench seats to avoid getting soaked, we start bailing.

Knowing I am tempting fate, I suggest the only thing missing is a fire to help us dry out. My friend becomes irresistibly seized by this idea. Ignoring any danger of asphyxiation or explosion, he crouches and lights the floorboards on fire.

IV. Open Book / Open to Interpretation

At an academic conference, the task at hand for the featured speaker is to explicate an ancient scroll decorated with runes.

The scroll is projected onto a screen above and behind him, text splayed wide.

But in his presentation, the man extrapolates freely, choosing to discuss instead the path to a *godly* life. I shake my head and ask questions incorporating as many magic symbols as possible, trying to get him to focus.

V. Surmounting Obstacles / Life's Journey

Our African guide speaks rapid-fire French. I struggle to adapt to his patois along with the other

Peace Corps volunteers.

We have made it over a high mountain pass and half-climbed, half-slid down to the remote village where I will soon lead a class of children as the new English teacher.

Already I'm wondering how to address the students, what to talk about. Fresh from my arduous journey, I reflect on the path that brought me here, the wide world beyond, and the notion that in their lives to come, the children may wish to retrace the same road to make their own discoveries.

I begin practicing the speech using the few words I know: *mountain*, *climb*, *difficult*, *journey*, *life*, and *begin*.

DREAMS OF THE DALAI LAMA

His Holiness the Dalai Lama was making an unscheduled appearance on campus. I happened to be in the auditorium with my daughter at just the right time. Spectators started entering en masse and the DL's staff stepped forward and began arranging them around the area where the leader would stand. Even though my daughter was no longer a child, the handlers must've liked the idea of filling in the crowd with young people—so there we were, stationed near the head of the line like solemn attendants at a wedding. Our college provost led the procession, offering me a limp handshake while dropping a catty comment about being surprised to see me there. Then the DL came out, pausing to smile and nod to my daughter and ask how I was doing. For some reason, I panicked and made an idle remark about meditating regularly. He continued down the line quickly, as if able to trace this falsehood on my face.

***

It was the Blessed One's funeral. Two ornate horse-pulled coaches waited on a side street near my apartment building followed by a line of buses.

Each carriage had been fitted with a decorative pagoda turret. A man emerged and announced over a bullhorn to pilgrims that buses would leave in five minutes. Until then, I hadn't considered attending this event myself. But I was too casually dressed and wished to retrieve my camera. To save time, I climbed the fire escape. Pressing my back against the building, I balanced along the ledge to my window, but found it locked. Below, the little caravan was just leaving.

***

Before me on a table were placed four objects. An old pair of wire frame glasses, a worn prayer book, a wooden begging bowl, and a comic book.

Select! I was instructed by a brusque-mannered junior monk. So I picked up the comic book and began reading.

You clearly aren't the Buddha of Compassion, he snorted. *Just what sort of Buddha are you?*

He made a gesture with his arm as if to dismiss me.

Wait, said the senior monk, stepping forward and grasping the junior one's sleeve. *That actually was one of His.*

THE WIKI DREAM INTERPRETER

Client: During our training for the world soccer tournament, Coach insisted on all of us getting a good night's sleep and laid down strict rules: no alcohol, no club parties, and no women. The first week, I had the strangest dream. We were playing against another team clothed in burkas and the players would tackle us whether we had the ball or not. Over subsequent nights, this competition grew more intense. Opposing players began grabbing at us, even pulling us to the ground and mounting us. In one dream, two months into the harsh training regimen, the player astride me pulled aside the veil to reveal the face of a well-known swimsuit model. The gown this woman wore slid partway open, revealing a pair of ripe, pendulant breasts. She then pressed her half-clothed body against mine; and in that moment, I . . . [*Content Deleted*].

Wiki Dream Interpreter: Fundamentally this is a dream about sports; which, as any online dictionary will tell you, is really about personal "goal"-setting (this may manifest itself literally, in a dream about soccer). The facial coverings of opposing players suggest the "veiling" of a personal issue you must confront and a certain degree of self-denial on your part regarding the importance of pursuing your objectives. I sense you're uncertain about this? Consider the dream a rallying cry to strip the mask off your present situation, to ask yourself the questions, "Who am I?" and, "What goals do I wish to achieve?"

Client: Sir, I took your advice and joined the zendo to get in touch with my inner self. But during periods of extreme fasting, I started obsessing over food. I was assured this was quite natural, but my cravings grew unbearable and haunted my sleep. I'd find myself transported back to my childhood home during a holiday feast, sometimes with the zen master himself sitting silently by, neither approving nor disapproving. Then came a dream in which he attempted to interpose himself between the banquet table and me. So I morphed into this huge gaping maw of a mouth and ate him, too.

Wiki Dream Interpreter: The presence of "comfort food" suggests a desire to return home, perhaps all the way back to the mother/master. In this context, your use of the word "maw" must be considered a pun. Cannibalism, however, always represents a destructive or forbidden desire, and in combination with other associations, suggests a fundamentally unhealthy relationship with your mother. There must be emotional issues which have gone unresolved for too long, which have left you feeling "starved"? Regard this dream as a clarion call to confront your mother, to stand up for yourself and insist, "Love me. Care for me. Feed my emotional needs."

Client: Sir, I have a question from my mother. Ever since I've moved back home, she's been having her own dream in which she's pregnant again (my mother is in her sixties and post-menopausal, so this is impossible) and the fetus has grown so big she has to lie on her back, not inside the house, but outside, for fear her abdomen could burst through the roof. She's embarrassed to be put on display in this manner in front of her neighbors, who aren't hesitant to query about her naked belly.

Wiki Dream Interpreter: Clearly, your mother fears she is going to be "exposed" to others, probably for a situation or state-of-affairs she wishes to keep hidden, or strictly among household "insiders." Do you have any idea what this shameful circumstance might be?

Client: Gosh, no. I've only been living at my mother's place for six months but can't imagine her harboring any secrets.

Wiki Dream Interpreter: A "secret" is not necessarily a bad thing: according to leading online dictionaries, it may symbolize power, or perhaps an emergent subconscious realization that while there's an unpleasant problem to face, one possesses the inner reserves to do so. Tell your mother to take this dream as a call to arms to expel the noxious influence from her life.

Client: That's great news, thanks!

Wiki Dream Interpreter: You're most welcome.

Client: May I ask you about my own dream, sir? Lately I've been hanging out at Starbucks when I've promised my mother I'll be out looking for work. I'll spend most of the day sipping coffee because I don't wish to return to more criticism. I'll be sitting in one of those plush chairs with my laptop and start to nod off. Soon I find myself transported back to ancient times, where I'm seated on a bench in a plaza next to a reflecting pool. Fountains gush from classical statues. One figure intrigues me: its stony countenance eerily resembles my own, and as I listen to the water trickling out below, I receive a lasting impression of contentment and peace. The position of the arms is also most striking: the one on the left hangs downward, like the David's; the one on the right is held akimbo, forming a kind of loop. From my vantage, the shape seems to spell out the letter "P." Please, could you tell me what this means?

Wiki Dream Interpreter: It means you have to pee.

THE CHURCH OF UNIVERSAL ENTROPY

To: Mitch Mallecho, Ph.D.

From: Klark Bulmer, IRS Taxpayer Advocate

Re: Recent Application for Recognition of Exemption

Date: April 21, 2014

Dear Dr. Mallecho,

Our office has reviewed, with careful attention, your recent fifty-seven page e-mail communication regarding the adverse determination made by the IRS Office with respect to your Application for Recognition of Exemption on behalf of the Church of Universal Entropy, of which you are sole founder.

We understand the rules governing exempt organizations can be complex, even frustrating, for anyone attempting to navigate them without the assistance of a certified tax preparer. And we regret to learn that the free taxpayer service available through the community center in your area was unable to assist with some of the vagaries of Form 1023.

Unfortunately, at this time, there remain several obstacles to classifying your church as a religious nonprofit.

1. Universality does not render an enterprise "religious" per se. To the extent you are disseminating the concept of entropy to others you are characterizing the operation of a thermodynamic process, and therefore providing an information service.

2. The cosmos may be trending toward entropy, which may spell our doom, but this eventuality is likely to be many billions of years away. For the short term, *quoad* the 2013 fiscal year, you acknowledge that you haven't maintained the ledgers or receipts needed to complete Form 1023.

3. Nor do you hold structured meetings with your followers, advocate a set of ritual practices, or offer any hope of salvation.

4. I am afraid our office cannot accept a rationale that the lack of orderliness in one's records stems from "a core belief in chaos itself."

5. With respect to your belief that society is in a period of profound decline, many of our

representatives are in sympathy, as they are with your examples of personal disappointments in business and academia. But the grounds for thinking this brand of cynicism rises to the level of an alternative belief system are less clear and would appear to derive an affirmative conclusion from negative premises.

6. We concede that your disengagement from current events is both genuine and endemic, and it is clearly a point in your favor that your church has never supported a political candidate or campaign. No longer having the energy to show up for work, however, might present to some as a reason for seeking career counseling, rather than as a ground for the claim that you are "The Earthly Incarnation of Entropy," notwithstanding the attached testimonies of your landlord and former wife.

7. It may be true, as you contend, that great religious leaders of history took little care for the world and felt "beholden to no conventions"; yet it seems inconsistent, or a case of special pleading, to then insist on one's status as the founder of a faith in order to reap the tax benefits. One way or another, we must render unto Caesar what is Caesar's.

8. Finally, if the rough numbers submitted for estimated revenues are accurate and the parishioners

at the soup kitchen you frequent have little or no money for donations, we question whether it is necessary, in this case, to file Form 1023 at all.

With all due respect, sir, the IRS is not a "heartless behemoth"; we are people willing to extend you and work with you, and I apologize again for your recent negative experience with our customer telephone hotline. Our representatives are not as conversant with quantum theory as they should be, but weren't incorrect to inform you that The Church of Universal Entropy does not meet the criteria for religious exemption at this time.

On a personal note, I wish you the best in your ongoing quest to better understand the cosmos, and to come to grips with the unpleasant fact that sometimes when we would wish to better order our relationships with others, we find ourselves left alone to deal with chaos.

PRAYER TO URANIA

The universal muse awaits her due,
Hungry for eyes to drift upward
From the shrines and holy cities
To the far reaches,

Where new galaxies spin like Sufis,
And quasars brighter than the stars of prophets
Gleam like votive offerings,
Making even the end of time seem mundane.

We must try to transcend
Our stunted perspective;
We must strive to become
Better wards of space.

Let us beseech the ozone layer for forgiveness.
Let us contemplate sacred mysteries of dark matter.
Let us pray for a sense of awe and a firm faith in science
That shall require no miracles to direct our gaze
    heavenward.

THE END OF DAYS

A Film Treatment

I. Opening Scroll

During the second century of the Third Millennium, the Earth became covered with toxic yellow clouds.

Despite last-ditch measures to eliminate greenhouse gasses, the atmosphere thickened, grew stagnant, and died. The planet's rotation slowed, and then stopped: Earth was tidally locked.

Thereafter, one side always faced the sun while the other remained shrouded in darkness.

Constant winds blew over the surface and people took shelter. And most of the population—plant, animal, and human—died out within a span of two days.

And Great Wars were fought over control of the temperate Middle Territories and stormy Shadowlands in-between.

Until the generations which had known night and day vanished, and the children who had grown up in light embraced the light, and the children who had grown up in darkness learned to embrace the darkness.

This time of peace became known as the End of Days.

II. Backstory

Over time, inhabitants of the Dark Side grew lighter skinned and inhabitants of the Light Side darker skinned. There were other evolutionary adaptations, too: in eyes, hair color and texture. Picture a native of Iceland residing on the Dark Side and a native of the Democratic Republic of the Congo on the Light Side, and you're probably not far off. Which is ironic, because when the globe stopped spinning, Reykjavik was left in full sunlight and most of East-Central Africa in the dark.

That was one good effect of Earth's tidal locking: racism was finally dead. It had taken evolution centuries to kill it—for a long time there, you still might have witnessed the spectacle of a blackened-skinned man blustering about white supremacy, or an albino-looking chap militating for Black Nationalism.

The Shadowlands stretched along the Prime Meridian, from Greenwich down through the now defunct countries of France, Algeria, Mali, Ghana, and Burkina Faso. The former capital city of Ouagadougou was considered by many the best, most desirable place in the world to live.

As the End of Days continued, people visited the Shadowlands less often. Constant storms served as a natural barrier to travel. Massive aqueducts had been constructed to channel runoff to deserts on the Light Side and pipelines built to convey tepid air to the Dark Side. Nobody had cause to venture there apart from scientific teams and repair crews. Or perhaps a rare artist or poet intrigued by the spectacular play of light and shadow.

III. Main Character: Axelle

Focus in on AXELLE, racing along the desert floor in her airbike. Touching up, touching down, hovering over rocky terrain. Dark braids spill out of her helmet, and underneath the visor is a face that is beyond beautiful.

Axelle is attuned to another screen on the inside of the visor as she drives. In her virtual world she cuts through jungle and jumps over nonexistent streams and chasms.

Out of the corner of her eye she sees a little red alert light, blinks twice, and the backdrop vanishes.

Ahead of her, a dark shelf cloud dominates the landscape. Below it, bright streaks of rain descend like a bamboo curtain.

Axelle approaches the edge of the squall line, not slowing. Although the atmospheric conditions create some interference with her navigational system (from a low angle of Axelle on her airbike, we can see faint crackles of heat lightning overhead), she grows bolder as she loops farther into the darkness.

She soars up and over a ditch easily, then another and another. The bike has one rough touchdown and Axelle struggles to retain control. But she enjoys the challenge, attempts daring jumps again and again. Until the bike lands near the edge of a fault line and she's catapulted forward.

Axelle hits the ground, rolls, and lies still.

We now get our first real look at the Shadowlands. It is a place of constant drizzle in which only a rare sunbeam passes through the cloud cover to create a mottled pool of twilight.

In this tidally locked Earth, the Shadowlands is the

only above-ground area any wildlife has survived, in the form of moors, twisted trees, and occasional bat-bird or swamp panther with oddly elongated legs. Black lakes harbor formerly mild-mannered aquatic creatures grown supersized and surly, as if forced to evolve with a gun at their heads.

Most noticeable of all are the surface winds, constantly blowing toward the sunlit side. For this reason, the bat-birds don't fly so much as soar, like kites caught in a storm.

IV. Main Character: Wasis

WASIS (Wuz for short) is a slender, pale-skinned young man of remote Senegalese descent who will eventually find Axelle. A geophysicist, he's commissioned to oversee the pipelines that conduct heat to Dark settlements, allowing life to go on.

Like everything in the Shadowlands, the pipeline has a tendency to break down. Wuz is currently out with a field crew repairing a leak thought to have been caused by a toxic combination of icy rain and bat-bird guano.

Axelle is not difficult for Wuz to spot, even in semi-darkness, in her silver cycling suit. Yet he's never seen anyone like her.

When she comes to, Axelle sees a Handsome Elf looking her way with concern. Her first thought is that the impact has switched on her helmet's TolkienWorld program. So she's surprised to discover her helmet off and the Elf gently bathing her forehead with a cool rag.

"You have a nasty bump there," the Elf tells her.

"You're not supposed to talk," Axelle retorts.

"Ah—I should probably ask you a few questions. You lost consciousness and may have a mild concussion. How's the vision?" the Elf asks, holding up two fingers.

"Not sure—that could be 'peace' or 'victory.'"

"Excellent! And your hearing?"

"You talk kind of like an android, you know."

"I get that from the guys on the pipeline. And what's your name?"

"That's confidential."

"Well—I'm glad you remember it's supposed to be confidential."

He paused. "I guess I'm out of questions."

"Axe."

"I can't think of anything else to ask!"

"No, my name is Axe. You just flunked the Turing Test, droid," she says, giving his hand holding the rag a playful twist.

"Ouch," Wuz says.

The two hit it off immediately, of course.

Wuz does most of the talking as Axe recuperates. He explains he's a recent Ph.D. who's been researching the Shadowlands. He takes Axe to a pipeline maintenance station and offers her a warm beverage that's a remote descendant of coffee, hydroponically grown and beaker-tasting, but with an absolutely wicked amount of caffeine.

Axe makes a face.

But revived by the java jolt, she breaks her silence. Axe is Commander-General of Light Military Forces, though since the End of Days has lasted for centuries, the post is nominal. She spends most of her time rock climbing and riding her bike through the desert when not laying into some underling at the military academy.

"That's impressive," Wuz says.

"You're not so bad yourself, Pinky."

V. Rising Arc

Over the following weeks, Axe and Wuz become friends. More than friends, actually. To write that they came from different worlds wouldn't be accurate (that romantic cliché never is)— but different half-worlds, yes. Natural selection, however, can't fully operate on beings raised for generations in an artificial environment. And so, even after centuries of divergence, the two remain the same species. No doubt about it.

Here are a few of Axe and Wuz's adventures together: a panther chase (catch-and-release); a fish-o-saur expedition (catch and retreat); a rock climb on the Light Side (Wuz is weighted down with specimens); and a tour of Great War battleground sites on the Dark Side (Axe grows a bit salty when Wuz's narration betrays his ignorance of military history).

They attempt a Shadowlands picnic that ends in a

rain-out and seek shelter in a lost parking garage, which leads to the ruins of a luxury hotel, where they spend a cozy, rather Gothic evening by torchlight— far more romantic than the original plan.

Neither knows how friends and family might react to the news they are together, so they keep their relationship a secret. There'd been no open hostilities for half a millennium, but there was always fear— enough to keep the armies well-funded.

Axe and Wuz agree that the rift is unfortunate. The two sides could learn from each other, and the Earth had been a beautiful place when darkness and light weren't permanent conditions—when all living things, unlike those miserable creatures roaming the Shadowlands, had a chance to flourish.

They had grown up, like all kids, in virtual play areas. The Old Earth videos made children beg their parents to be allowed out, just once, believing recognizable traces of the environment must still be there. You can imagine their disappointment after being bundled up and sent out to have a look. The Shadowlands was the place teenage friends still dared each another to visit—at least, until the first threatening funnel cloud called an end to such hijinks. Afterwards, young people were usually content to subsist indoors, which was a problem for several reasons. First, it left them soft and doughy: Axe found whipping recruits into shape grew harder each year. Second, high-tech toys left them too complacent to become inventors themselves: technology remained totally last-century. Last, it led to overpopulation.

Unlike wild animals, human beings never had much difficulty breeding in captivity. In fact, they did rather a lot of it. Government officials who'd remained forward-looking enough to recognize this problem warned the planet might be stripped of resources all over again.

That's why citizens of the Light and Dark Sides had resumed pointing fingers in each other's direction. When things grew scarce, the easiest solution wasn't to cut back, but to wage war against those perceived hoarders and wasters on the other side.

The anti-other feeling had recently begun to crest. Axe is particularly concerned because she knows that buried in underground silos in the Shadowlands are enough nuclear warheads to destroy the planet several times over.

Centuries before, at the cessation of the last Great War, both sides had laid down arms in neutral territory, sealed them up, and walked away.

VI. Subplot That Will Later Intersect

As their relationship deepens, Wuz describes for Axe his doctoral thesis. His research led him to the conclusion that Earth's tidal locking provided a natural countermeasure to the greenhouse gases which had caused it to stop spinning in the first place. The lock generated constant hot and cold fronts across the planet that worked like giant rollers, wringing out CO_2 from the atmosphere. Shadowlands storms supplied a rinse cycle, siphoning air up and into space.

True, Earth's atmosphere was being stripped of oxygen also, and that little situation was becoming critical; but after all, the Dark Side was mostly ice. If the planet started moving again, the ice would thaw and the air could begin to replenish itself. And plants would be the first form of life to spread out from the Shadowlands, regenerating even more O_2.

Wuz had taken atmospheric measurements from skyscrapers on the Dark Side to test his theory— and more recently, during the climb on the Light Side with Axe. There, too, the planet's air tested crystalline pure.

"So why aren't we spinning again?" asks Axe.

"Momentum doesn't come from nothing," Wuz says. "We need a push as well as a pull."

"Oh," says Axe, suddenly interested.

"Right now, the Earth is getting a little nudge from the moon. But the moon is pulling against the sun, so the planet isn't going to budge. Theoretically, if an asteroid came along and hit Earth a glancing blow, enough to create a decent torque vector, it could provide enough thrust to get the ball rolling."

Axe winced. She'd warned Wuz about the science nerd puns.

"Unfortunately, you can't precision-tune an asteroid," he added.

But Axe seems to have lost focus on his words, or is thinking about something else entirely.

"How many megatons in an asteroid?" she asks.

VII. Complications

Axe tells Wuz about the missiles in Shadowlands bunkers and he recognizes a potentially significant amount of firepower in thousands of rocket thrusters. Hypothetically, it might not be necessary to explode the nukes—at least, not more than a few.

What neither of them knows is the same stockpile of weapons is being discussed by the powers-that-wished-to-be on both sides. Even though Axe was military leader of half the globe, she'd openly ridiculed the idea of a territorial grab and was now being branded antiwar. Fortunately, there'd been no discovery of her relationship with Wuz, or that day's closed-door meeting at Light Side Military HQ would've ended in a coup.

Simultaneously, on the Dark Side, leaders were also meeting (one must resist calling them the Powers of Darkness), drawing similar conclusions about the inevitability of war and entertaining a motion to send troops to the Shadowlands to check on weapon security. The warheads lay buried in the heart of the region, at a site known as the Dunes.

The Dunes crossed a fault line at the former Prime Meridian—the perfect site for placing a lever, Wuz reflects. He's been thinking of Archimedes' words: *Give me a lever long enough and a fulcrum on which to place it and I shall move the world.* Logistically, depending on the positioning of the missiles, Operation Push actually seems viable to him.

So Wuz and Axe make plans for an expedition the next day. Axe to borrow an amphibious vehicle stocked with provisions and gear, Wuz to fetch digging tools.

Neither fully anticipates the hard slog ahead. Axe checks out of the base early enough to avoid raising suspicions, although she's detained at the gate slightly longer than her patience lasts.

She later picks up Wuz at their rendezvous, but very soon they encounter a storm, two funnel clouds that spin toward them like buffers at a car wash.

Somehow, they manage to squeeze through.

Next they find themselves in a bog so thick the vehicle is stuck. To make matters worse, as they slog ahead on foot, they're attacked by a ginormous creature that surfaces with wide-open mouth, a cross between a carp's and a crocodile's.

Axe fires until the monster submerges.

From this point they dodge a forest of brambles and a spindly-legged panther or two, but finally arrive at the Dunes just as a military plane circles overhead.

Now why didn't I think of that? is Axe's first thought.

She recognizes the plane as one of Wuz's side's.

"Don't look at me," he says.

"It's a drone," she explains. "If it's scouting ahead, your boys won't be far behind."

Moments later, Axe and Wuz spot a mysterious cowled figure who steps from a stand of cypresses to block their path.

This giant has a gaunt countenance with deep-sunken eyes. He stands guard over the site like one of the priests of Nemi, challenging that the only way to pass is to defeat him in mortal combat and thereby become his successor.

Wuz tries to explain their mission, but the Dune Priest only pulls out a cruel-looking sword and gives it a flourish.

Wuz stands down.

"Got another one of those, Pops?" asks Axe, removing her helmet so she'll have no unfair advantage.

At the sight of her face, the Dune Priest reacts as though he's beheld the goddess Diana herself. Until he hears Axe say, "Never mind, this'll do."

She picks up a dead tree limb and wields it overhead like a club.

The two circle each other. The Dune Priest makes a couple of swift passes, but in a lightning counterattack Axe puts him on the ground.

"Yield," she demands, theatrically. "Your time as guardian has passed; by decree, mine must begin. I grant you your life in return for the secret knowledge you must impart about this site to myself and no other."

She picks up the man's sword, tossing it to Wuz: "Take this, Pale Slave."

The Dune Priest, dazed, stands up; then confused, prostrates himself on the ground before Axe. *Make up thy mind*, she thinks, but doesn't say anything out loud, realizing she's just shattered this man's whole raison d'être and he certainly hasn't been paying into a retirement plan.

The Dune Priest leads Axe and Wuz through the cypress grove, down through a rocky gorge to the entrance to a tunnel.

He takes a torch from a wall (a primitive energy source, but readily renewable in a swamp). The two are relieved to see the blasted rock of the tunnel give way to masonry and steel.

Visible just ahead is an elevator. They pause.

"Doesn't work," the Dune Priest barks. "This way."

He leads them through a door to a steel circular staircase which descends as far as they can see.

"I go no further," he adds. "Bad knees."

VIII. The Crisis Reached

Down Axe and Wuz climb, their way lit by emergency lights. They've completed countless dizzying circumnavigations and Wuz is breathing heavily.

"Wheezy Wuzzie," Axe teases.

"Halt!" comes a commanding voice from above.

"Time to move," Axe urges, taking Wuz's arm.

Shots ring out, pinging off the steel staircase.

Axe and Wuz begin an all-out race down the staircase as the Dark Troops continue to fire. Due to the angle of descent there's little danger of being hit, but a few bullets ricochet too close for comfort.

The troopers realize they're losing out by just standing in place and firing. They set off in pursuit at a fast march.

Axe has to more-or-less drag Wuz the rest of the way.

At the bottom of the staircase she manages to muscle open a thick steel door that hasn't budged in centuries. Which she then reseals and bolts from inside, buying as much time as she can.

Wuz slowly gets his bearings. They are in the control room of an old military base deep in an underground cavern.

Thousands of missiles are siloed off to one side, stuck into the rock wall like bones in a catacomb.

"Excellent!" he murmurs.

He applies himself to the task of restoring the power grid, which he's not long in doing. Lights pop on everywhere and the control panel starts to power up.

"That was easy—old-school technology," he tells

an appreciative Axe. "But getting those nukes back online is going to take some time."

"That's sort of my line," she replies, stepping over to help. "And I think we've got a couple of hours. Those sad sacks out there are going to try forcing the door, realize they can't, probably try shooting at it, realize that's no good, then scramble back up those stairs and return with an explosive strong enough to rip through a six-foot steel door—

"—which, by the way, was designed to be bomb-proof."

"And still is?"

"Pa-leeze. I don't know about you guys, but we have mega lasers that could easily take it out."

"We might be trapped on the Dark Side, but we're not in the Dark Ages."

"The less braggin', the less draggin'."

"Oorah!"

IX. Climax and Falling Arc

They settle into their tasks. Wuz's fingers fly over the controls while Axe roams the missile bay to check all the thrusters.

An hour or two later, Operation Push is essentially in place.

It comes time to commence the countdown, but a final obstacle presents itself.

The plan had been to start a twenty-four hour clock, flee the Shadowlands, and escape to the safety of a Light Side bunker. Not even Wuz was exactly clear how great the aftershock would be; he just knew Earth was going to get a very big push.

"How much time?" Wuz asks Axe.

"Give us two hours. Then we'll open the door, surrender, and say we're out of oxygen or something. Or better, tell them we've discovered the whole site is dangerously contaminated."

"Did I mention, I found the circuit to turn on the elevator?"

"Idiot."

The two do in fact choose the escape option over the surrender option or the waiting-to-be-blown-up option.

When they burst out of the elevator, the Dark Side troops are somewhere in mid-staircase, lugging something that looks like a giant frosting gun.

Axel finds it easy to grab the weapon from the surprised sentry in the hallway and drag him to one of the waiting helicopters, which she has no trouble in commandeering.

She holds a gun to the captured soldier's head and threatens to shoot him unless the pilot takes off immediately.

The pilot complies, clearly in awe of her.

Just as the helicopter rises, Axe kicks her captive out the side. "Send word to your buddies to drop whatever they're doing and get the hell out of there. The tops of those Dunes are about to be blown off."

"Sorry to give that guy the bum's rush," she remarks candidly to Wuz a moment later, "and I've forgiven them all for shooting at us. If they were killed in action now, it'd seem like senseless collateral damage."

X. Epilogue: The End of the End of Days

There is a muted explosion, a jolt, a judder, and then a slow pulling away as the planet starts moving again.

Suddenly cast in light, the Shadowlands don't look so haunting. Mournful, perhaps, or simply lonesome for more life.

Things will never be quite the same: this New Earth will turn more slowly, each day lasting as long as three Old Earth days. But the major arc dividing day and night will never stop gliding across its surface.

On the formerly Dark side, residents will rise to go outdoors and notice ice on the rooftops beginning to melt, drip, and hit the snow below. Somewhere beneath, the deep-frozen turf is waiting to rebound.

On the formerly Light Side, a soothing shadow spreads across the desert, and there people will step outside too, and stretch and grow sleepy, but not before glancing up at the night sky, unseen for centuries.

And they will discover that, like so many other things in life, those stars really do possess more magic, seen live.

AFTERWORD

We are all the sons of our works, as Don Quixote most sanely observed. But literary works are themselves foundlings, and to establish their parentage is to retrace an almost impossible Ariadne's thread. At the same time, I don't wish to forsake my literary fathers as callously as Theseus, who abandoned his benefactress on the island of Naxos.

The references to made-up cults interwoven through pieces such as "A Brief History of Vigilism" or "The Biggest Man in the Universe" owes something to Calvino; subtitling two pieces "Tales for Children" is a trick learned from Marquez. But the true father of this book may be Jorge Luis Borges, whose paternal influence over the stories "Daniel L. Erst, Inventor of the Multiverse Helmet" and "The Ibis" I dutifully acknowledge.

Even in composing this Afterword, I find myself recalling one of Borges' own prologues, in which he writes that all literature is "guided dreaming." The world of quantum particles is purely mathematical; my take on it, metaphorical. In writing this book, I consulted several texts such as Cox and Forshaw's

The Quantum Universe, if only to glean more ideas to dream upon.

Just to illustrate in a quantum universe, accidents predictably occur: the made-up book review "A Brief History of Vigilism" was written before I read that Carl Sagan famously directed one of the Voyagers to turn its camera around to capture an image which would later inspire his book *Pale Blue Dot*.

And so I shall claim him, somewhat after the fact, for a Vigilist.

ACKNOWLEDGMENTS

"Another Version of Purgatory" first appeared in *The Literati Quarterly*; "The Astronaut Diet" in *Pure Coincidence Magazine*; "The Biggest Man in the Universe" in *Common Oddities Speculative Fiction Sideshow*; "The Box of Space" in *Lowestoft Chronicle*; "The Church of Universal Entropy" in *Scintilla*; "Daniel L. Erst, Inventor of the Multiverse Helmet" in *Little Patuxent Review*; "Dream Metaphors" in the *Journal of Microliterature*; "A Glossary of Lost Cults" in *Carbon Culture Review*; and "Retracing My Steps" in *Spark*. Thanks to the editors of some of these publications for their comments and suggestions on earlier versions of the stories.

About the Author

M.V. Montgomery is a professor at Life University in Atlanta. His books include the Winter Goose titles *What We Did with Old Moons*, *Beyond the Pale,* and *A Dictionary of Animal Symbols*.